CHAPTER ONE

Anders Nordic, a big, rawboned, blond-bearded Norwegian American from Dakota Territory, felt a hot curl of air off his right ear.

An eyewink later, the bullet slammed loudly into a tree bole just ahead and to Nordic's right, followed another eyewink later by the thundering report of the rifle that had fired it. His barrel-chested Appaloosa, Apache—named after the only people the devout people hater really admired—reared, whinnied, and took off like he had just sniffed wildfire behind him. A pine bough lay just ahead of Nordic, coming up fast as the stallion broke into a dead run. Anders shucked his 1866 Winchester "Yellowboy" repeater from his saddle scabbard, dropped it to the grassy ground, then flung both arms straight above his head.

The pine bough slammed into them, on the inside of his elbows, and he hooked both arms around it, letting the limb slide him quickly though easily out of the saddle to hang there a second, head reeling, before dropping straight down to the ground. Nordic's boon companion, a shaggy collie named Finn, stood several yards off in the trees to Anders's right, eyes glassy with fear, tongue drooping over his lower jaw, tail sagging, gazing off in the direction from which the shot had come.

Nordic had dropped, bending his knees to distribute the blow. Now he straightened and ran crouching back to where his Yellowboy lay in the grass. He picked up his prized weapon and, as another bullet hummed eerily toward him to tear up grass and sage only a few feet to his right, he yelled, "Come on, Finn!" and took off running into the thick pines ahead and on his left.

Finn didn't need to be told twice.

The collie had been with his pal, Nordic, only a few months, but before he'd been rescued, he'd been alone and homeless in the violent town of Cimarron in the New Mexico Territory and hounded and teased by a pack of nasty little boys. Finn knew his rescuer attracted bullets the way some men attracted money or women. In other words, this wasn't his first rodeo. The dog ran along beside the big man from Dakota as they made their way together toward a low stone escarpment fifty yards away, the ground between them narrowing quickly.

Nordic was six foot four with yoke-like shoulders, but he was fleet as a deer. At least, when he needed to be. Now, with some SOB bearing down on him with a rifle for whatever reason—he was pretty sure of the reason but there was no point in dwelling on that now

—he needed to be. Two more bullets caromed in, one thudding into the ground just behind his right boot, another into an aspen bole just ahead and on his left, spraying bark in all directions.

The thundering reports of the rifle came from behind him maybe sixty yards to the west.

Finn gained the rocks well ahead of Nordic, leaping into them and hunkering low. As another bullet chewed up turf to Anders's right, he dove forward over the first low wall of rock, struck on a clear area beyond, rolled, then rose to his haunches and threw himself behind a wall of rock maybe six feet high, to the right of Finn, who hunkered belly down, panting, eyes glassy.

"Not sure I done gave you the biggest favor, adoptin' you," the big man said now, doffing his cream felt *sombrero* and tossing it down at his side. His deep voice was lightly touched with a Scandinavian accent, for his parents had been born in their home country and he had grown up speaking Norwegian. "I know what you're thinkin'. Hell, I'd be thinkin' the same thing. You mighta leaped from the fryin' pan into the fire!"

He snorted a laugh at that.

Of course, Finn didn't understand what he'd said. Or maybe he had. The dog was uncannily wise and intuitive. For whatever reason, whether out of agreement or dissent, he looked at Nordic and gave a single, low bark.

"Yeah, I figured as much," Anders said with another wry chuckle. "You just like my cookin'!"

He edged a look around the right side of the bulging rock before him. Through the scattered ponderosas and firs of this high Colorado mountain country—the Never Summer Mountains north of Camp Collins, to be exact—another escarpment jutted out from the side of a pine-covered ridge roughly sixty, seventy feet away. Atop the scarp he could see a man's hatted head hunkered over a rifle barrel. Sunlight winked off the barrel and, sensing another shot was imminent, Nordic pulled his head back behind his rocky cover.

Sure enough, an eyewink later the bullet slammed against the rock with a thunderous roar followed by a whipping report of the dry-gulcher's rifle.

Just before he'd pulled his head back, Nordic thought he'd spied the crowns of two more hats, meaning there were at least three men out to snuff his wick atop that scarp. He was pretty sure he knew who they were. A half hour ago, he and Finn were trotting along the old woodcutter's trail near the base of North Diamond Peak, scouting the free-range country run by Garth Deveraux, for whom Anders worked, and manning a small line shack just a few miles southwest of here and on which Deveraux, an Englishman, grazed his Herefords. Nordic had met three men on the trail—a stone-faced, rugged, mysterious lot clad in wolfskin or bearskin coats. It was cold this high in the appropriately named Never Summers even in midsummer, as it was now. The three men, all beefy and bearded and owning the flat expressions of wily outlaws, eyed him suspiciously, saying nothing as they'd passed on by Nordic and Finn.

Nordic had said nothing in return. They weren't the types you exchanged pleasantries with.

When he had moved on another twenty yards, he glanced behind him to see one of them hipping around to look at him, as well. The man turned quickly forward and then all three disappeared down a low declivity into heavy forest, gone.

In this remote country, they were likely the only three other men besides Nordic out here. They'd likely circled around him and climbed the scarp they were shooting from now.

Why?

Rustlers.

They'd likely long looped several of Deveraux's beeves and had them penned up in a box canyon somewhere.

They were the reason Nordic was up here, manning that line shack. To watch after the Englishman's herds. Rustlers were a dime a dozen in these parts. Nordic had shot four in just the two months he'd been up here already.

Another bullet hammered the rock he and Finn hunkered behind. When the echo of the rifle's report had dwindled to silence, a man's voice yelled in the distance, "Come on out an' we'll make it quick, Dakota!"

"Dakota, huh?" Nordic said with a whimsical air. "I don't remember meetin' those fellas, but they sure know who I am, all right." The reputation of a big man like Nordic, especially who'd killed men up here and been in trouble in town, preceded him. Damn it, anyway!

Word had somehow gotten out that Deveraux had hired a big Scandinavian-American from Dakota Territory to man his line camp. This country was sparsely populated, the large ranches spread good distances apart. Still, cowpunchers and rustlers and miners and woodcutters alike gathered in the little town of Camp Collins at the eastern base of the range and in the several road ranches peppered around the mountains' high valleys.

Nordic didn't respond.

He'd leave them up there, wondering if he was still here behind this low mound of jumbled rock. He looked around, trying to figure a way out of his predicament. He couldn't wait here because eventually they'd come down and flush him out. He couldn't leave his fate in their hands. He had to do something himself.

Looking around, his gaze landed on the creek he'd crossed just before he'd been shot at. It traced a horseshoe curve around him, beyond pines, cedars, and aspens maybe thirty yards away. He glanced around his covering rock once more, giving a quick look at the scarp atop which his dry-gulchers lay. He pulled his head back quickly then looked at the creek again. If he ran toward it, he might be seen from that scarp. There were enough scattered trees and rocks to offer cover, however. He'd just as soon gain the creek without them knowing it. He'd like to work around behind them. If they saw him, they'd figure out what he was up to.

He decided it was worth the risk.

There was going to be shooting no matter what he did. He'd just like to try to edge the odds a little closer to his side of the table, though.

Hefting the Yellowboy in both his gloved hands, he rose to a crouch, keeping his head down below the lip of his covering rock. He glanced at the dog lying belly down beside him, panting, eyeing him expectantly, likely wondering how in hell his master—if Anders was, indeed, his master—was going to get them out of the current frying pan they found themselves in and not into the fire.

"Let's go, Finn. Nice an' quiet, pard!"

CHAPTER TWO

Nordic ran toward the creek cutting through the trees.

As he did, he traced a zigzagging route, running from tree to rock from rock to tree and back again until he and Finn pushed through shrubs and leaped down into the creek. Nordic's boots slipped off the rocks. The water, extremely cold at these climes, rose to just below his knees, sliding over and around rocks, making small rapids. It was relatively slow-moving now in midsummer—the water inky black and as cold as snowmelt.

Nordic knew it to be a good fishing stream. He'd taken several trout out of these cold waters, fishing deep pools and tree snags. He'd taken the fish home, cleaned them, and pan-fried them over an open fire just off the ancient line shack's sagging front porch, eating them with coffee liberally laced with whisky distilled locally by an old Scot prospector he'd met and who had a mining claim in a canyon near Owl Mountain.

He moved up the creek, Finn wading and swimming along beside him, occasionally leaping onto the bank when there was a ledge wide enough to hold him. At its widest, it wasn't wide enough to hold Anders. The water was damn cold, too cold for man or beast. The dog was damned loyal, Nordic would give him that. Too loyal. When he'd expunged the dry-gulching rustlers from his trail, he'd build him and his loyal companion a large, hot fire and feed him bacon from his saddlebags—when he found Apache again, that was.

As he made his way downstream, shivering, holding the Yellowboy up high across his chest, he felt optimistic. When he'd run from his covering rock to the creek, no bullets had caromed his way. He hoped that meant his dry-gulchers hadn't seen his move and figured his ploy.

As he continued downstream, following one bend in the creek after another, he kept an eye on the escarpment he could see through the pines and aspens lining the shore on his right. Gradually, as he kept wading, the scarp shifted from ahead on his right to behind his right shoulder. He waded another hundred yards then, tugging on roots looping up out of the shoreline, pulled himself up onto the bank.

Finn lay on the bank, in a patch of ferns, wet and panting and keeping his expectant brown eyes on the big, curious man who'd adopted him.

"Come on, Finn," Nordic said, shivering, looking forward to that fire. "Let's clear our trail, shall we?"

He'd taken only three steps toward the backside of the escarpment when Finn stopped suddenly and growled, raising his hackles.

Nordic spied movement just ahead, as a big, fur-clad man stepped out from behind a boulder. The man raised an old-model Spencer repeater to his shoulder and aimed down the barrel. Nordic threw himself to his left just as the Spencer thundered, sending a .56-caliber ball hurling over the creek behind him.

Finn yipped and growled, hunkered low, showing his teeth.

Nordic rolled onto his left shoulder, levered a round into the Yellowboy's action, and fired. The big man grunted and stumbled back three steps, lowering the Spencer with one hand, and looked down at the hole in his bear coat, over his heart. Long, stringy brown hair hung down over the hole, turning red as blood bubbled up out of it. He lifted his chin, looked at Nordic. He looked more animal than man with his tangled bear fur, flat brown eyes, and a thick wedge of a nose.

He grunted and tried to raise the Spencer again with his right hand but couldn't manage it. The rifle dropped from his hand to clatter onto the ground. The man stumbled back again. His eyes rolled up in his head and then he fell flat on his back without breaking his fall, dead before he hit the ground.

Finn growled again and then walked over and lifted his leg on the man's right leg.

Quickly levering another round into the Winchester's breech, Nordic gained his knees. He looked around cautiously, expecting to see the two other dry-gulchers moving out from surrounding firs, pines, and spruces. No movement. The only sound was the breeze and the cawing of crows that had lit from a near spruce when Nordic's Yellowboy had spoken and were winging off to the north.

Nordic rose slowly, surveying the area around him, shivering from his wet denims below the knees.

"Come on, Finn," he said quietly. "Nice and slow like."

The dog gave a shake, ridding its fur of more of the chill water, and then followed close on its master's heels as Nordic moved forward, holding his Winchester straight out from his right hip in one hand. As he closed on it, the escarpment grew before him. He moved into open ground between him and the formation. He was too close to it now to be seen from on top of it.

Good.

Since the other two dry-gulchers didn't seem to be anywhere near—if they were, he'd likely know it by now—they must still be on top of it, waiting. They sent one of them down here in case Nordic was trying to work around them. They'd heard the shot for sure. Now they were wondering who would join them at the top of the scarp—their partner or "Dakota."

At the base of the scarp, Nordic stopped to give it close scrutiny. The backside was the easiest way up, for it was mainly just a steep slope strewn with pines and boulders. Not a hard climb. That would be the route they'd expect him to take, if it was him who was coming, that was.

The front would be the toughest way up, for it was steeper and strewn with large boulders he'd have to climb over.

That was the way he'd go.

It was not a climb for a dog.

"Finn, stay here."

The dog looked at him, his expression showing dismay.

"I'll be back soon, an' I'll build us a fire."

The dog moaned and then dropped slowly to his belly and crossed his paws straight out in front of him.

"Attaboy."

He set his rifle down against a pine. He couldn't hold it and climb at the same time. He'd have to rely on the bone-gripped .44 holstered high on his right thigh.

Nordic chose a route then started up the steep incline, tracing a meandering course as he leaped up and over boulders and then climbed between them, grabbing for purchase gnarled cedars and stunt pines growing out of the face of the slope. He moved quickly, adeptly. He hailed from the rolling prairie, but he'd lived in the mountains long enough—mainly alone in isolated line shacks, which was the best life for a man who'd never gotten along well with others—that he'd become accustomed to perilous climbs usually while hunting or on the scout for rustlers, as he was now.

Fifteen minutes after he'd started the climb, he found himself ten feet from the crest of the ridge. He moved to the right of a dimpled round boulder and took two more steps up the incline. Now he found himself within three feet of the ridge crest. He grabbed the rocky lip of the ridge and, with a grunt, started to hoist himself up onto it when a shadow slid over the stone to his right.

A man's worn, high-topped boot appeared just inches ahead of him. Then the other boot appeared. Nordic slid his gaze up from the mule-eared boots and up, up across baggy, smoke-stained buckskin trousers and up, up over a gray wolfskin coat over which a buckskin tobacco pouch hung from a braided rawhide thong to the long, narrow, hollow-cheeked face carpeted by a thick, red-brown beard, the lines in the man's weathered face dark with soot and grime. The man's two dark hazel eyes narrowed and his lips stretched back from chipped, tobacco-brown teeth as he gave a foxy smile and slid the barrel of his Henry repeating rifle to within inches of Nordic's face.

The man's buckskin-gloved right thumb ratcheted back the hammer.

Nordic raised his thick, muscular right arm and slammed it sideways across the man's lower legs, chopping both feet out from under him. He gave a startled grunt and triggered the Henry skyward as he struck the ground hard on his back.

Nordic hoisted himself onto the ridge and, setting his knees beneath him, grabbed both the big man's feet in his arms and jerked the big man toward him then past him and over the lip of the ridge and onto the steep slope below. The man rolled ten feet—his long, red-brown hair jostling wildly around his head. He rolled up against the base of a boulder ten feet downslope, a pained expression on his bearded face.

Holding both arms high, he peered between them, scowling in shock and exasperation at the big man— every bit as big as himself—scowling back at him. Nordic unsheathed his .44, clicked the hammer back, and shot the big man twice in the chest. The man's head slammed back against the boulder then sagged to the ground as he died with a rattling sigh.

Nordic whipped around, cocking the smoking Colt and extending it straight out before him.

Two down, one to go.

Where was the third dry-gulching SOB?

"Where are you?" Nordic called, his voice echoing around the rocks and pines mantling the top of the scarp. "I know you're up here." He grinned. "Come on out. I'll make it quick!"

He rose slowly, moved slowly forward along the slanting crest of the ridge toward its backside. The very top of the ridge was barren—only an undulating floor of solid rock that had likely once been lava from some volcano that had blown its top millions of years before. Twenty yards from the lip of the ridge, the stone floor tapered off to a thin crust of dirt carpeted in needles and cones dropped from the pines so hardy and determined that Nordic had seen them growing out of tiny fissures in solid rock—on the steep sides of stone mountains, no less.

A man could learn a lot about tenacity and toughness from such unlikely examples as trees.

He only vaguely reflected on that now.

The brunt of his mind was on that third dry-gulcher. Nordic knew the man was here somewhere. Anders could feel his eyes on him, watching and waiting until he became a clear target among the trees, low-hanging boughs, scattered rocks, and small boulders. He'd walked maybe twenty yards from the solid stone mantling the ridge crest when a squirrel ahead and to his right began chittering loudly, furiously.

Anders stepped behind a pine to his left just as a bullet chewed into the pine's face, where he would have been a split second ago if he'd kept walking. He edged a look around the tree in time to see a short, stocky man in a long fox-skin coat step out from behind a pine twenty feet to Nordic's right. The man gritted his teeth inside his bearded face and narrowed his eyes as he aimed down the long-barreled Remington .44 in his gloved right hand.

A shadow moved downslope on the man's right. Snarling and growling rose, and then Finn leaped off his back feet and closed his jaws around the wrist of the man wielding the Remington. The revolver roared, smoke and flames lapping from the barrel. The bullet drilled into the pine just inches from Nordic's face. The man had had him dead to rights…before Finn had fouled his aim.

Hanging from the man's wrist by his jaws, Finn growled savagely and shook his head. The man screamed and fell to his right, screaming, "No! No! *Noooo!*"

Finn released the man's wrist then leaped onto his back, tearing into the back of the howling man's neck.

Heart thudding, knowing how close he'd been to shaking hands with the devil, Nordic stepped out from behind his covering pine and walked toward the enraged dog and the howling rustler.

"That's enough, Finn!" he called.

The dog removed his teeth from the back of the dry-gulcher's neck and looked at Anders, the savage fury still bright in his eyes.

"That's enough, boy," Nordic said. "I'll take it from here."

The dog barked, leaped off the man's back and sat down several feet away, facing the man and Nordic, who just then kicked the sobbing man over on his back. He clutched his bloody right hand and wrist in his left one, pinching his eyes closed and rolling his head in agony. He opened his eyes. They glinted with rage and misery as he bellowed, "Crazy, wild cur!"

Nordic planted one booted foot on the man's chest, cocked his Colt, and aimed at the man's ruddy, freckled forehead above his close-set eyes. "Where's the cattle?"

"What cattle?" the man bellowed, spittle flying from his lips.

Nordic extended the Colt closer to the man's head. "Wrong answer."

CHAPTER THREE

Nordic tossed another dry pine branch onto the fire he'd built in the trees not far from where the third dead man lay with a .44-caliber hole in his forehead.

Anders didn't fool around with dry-gulchers or rustlers. This man was both. If he'd not been, there would have been no need to clear the man they knew was working for Garth Deveraux out of this stretch of the Never Summers, which was Deveraux's traditional summer graze. Deveraux, like all ranchers, wanted Nordic to hang rustlers, but Nordic wouldn't do that. You had to be a particular brand of savage to hang a man.

Nordic was uncompromising and vicious when riled, but he could not bring himself to play cat's cradle with a man's head. A bullet would do. True, it was quicker, and it did not leave as dramatic a message to other would-be rustlers, but that was the only punishment Nordic was willing to inflict.

He'd done the third dry-gulcher a favor by drilling a bullet through the man's head when he'd refused to tell Anders where he'd find the cattle they'd stolen. It turned out he really didn't have to tell him. Just before Nordic had pulled the Colt's trigger, he'd heard the low of a distant cow, and then another. They weren't your usual lows. They were the lows of distressed stock likely pinned up somewhere nearby.

He'd locate and free them after he and Finn had warmed up and dried out by the fire.

Finn lay in a tight ball near the stone-ringed blaze, nose to tail, eyes soft with comfort. Anders stretched out near the dog, soaking in the heat from the snapping, crackling flames. He leaned back against a tree and, arms crossed on his chest, hat brim tugged down over his eyes, caught forty winks before waking and finding that his pants were all but dry.

He shoved his hat up on his forehead, lay another dry deadfall on the fire, and placed a hand on Finn's head. "You stay by the fire, boy. I'm gonna fetch Apache."

The dog lay as before, nose to tail, dozing. He looked up at Nordic then closed his eyes and gave a deep, contented sigh.

Nordic walked back through the trees to the stone-floored crest of the escarpment. He stood at the lip of the ridge overlooking the forest valley below—dark, jagged peaks rising in the far distance—removed a glove, and stuck two fingers between his lips. He gave a three-note whistle, which echoed around the valley, and waited.

Apache must have wandered back toward where he'd left his rider hanging from that pine bough because it was only about five minutes or so before the horse appeared at the base of the ridge, reins hanging, looking up at his rider standing on the ridge crest.

Nordic gave one more whistle and tossed his head to the right. The horse galloped off in the direction his rider had indicated.

Anders returned to the fire and stood soaking up the heat again, finishing the drying out of his denims. A few minutes later, Apache came galloping up the slope from the west, reins bouncing on the ground beside him. The horse ran to within six feet of its rider and jerked his head up and down, happily snorting and stomping.

Finn heard the horse's approach and raised his head. He regarded Apache warmly and thumped his tail.

All three, including the man, were content. They were all together again.

Nordic tightened Apache's cinch, reloaded both his pistol and rifle, slid the Yellowboy into its sheath, and swung up into the leather. To both the horse and the dog, he said, "Let's go free some beef and head on home. Gettin' late. Suppertime soon!"

He booted Apache on down the slope to the west. Fifteen minutes later, following the ever-loudening lows shepherded to his ears by the wind, he found the cattle penned in a small box canyon, branches and logs used as a makeshift gate across the canyon mouth. He ripped away the "gate," tossing the branches and logs in the brush, and the dozen or so Herefords—mostly cow-calf pairs—went running to freedom, the mothers kicking out their back legs, the calves playfully mounting each other.

Finn sat beside Nordic and barked. The cows' enthusiasm was catching.

Nordic watched them go, grinning.

He loved being out here in the wild with just the animals. Only humans ruined the serenity. There were three fewer of them now, left where they'd died, each one a meal for the buzzards, coyotes, and mountain lions. They needed to eat, too.

Thinking of eating, the big man's belly growled. He'd been too cold to cook bacon. The sun was sinking toward the western ridges. Shadows were long. He had a good hour's ride back to the cabin. He swung up into the leather and booted Apache northwest across the broad, sage-stippled valley. When after a half hour he gained the creek—if it had a name, he didn't know what it was—he swung north and followed the creek until it swung toward him. Then he crossed it, rode up and over a steep, pine-carpeted ridge and into the next valley on the other side.

Here his shack sat along yet another creek. He didn't know its name, either, if it had one. There was a creek to every valley and there must have been thousands of canyons and valleys in the Never Summers. The cabin was a humble log, low-swung hovel with a shake roof green with moss and peppered with leaves and small branches a recent wind had blown off the surrounding pines, firs, and aspens.

Finn ran up onto the small, roofed front porch to sniff the iron pot Nordic used to feed him, though he didn't have to feed the dog much. Finn was a good hunter and sustained himself with rabbits and squirrels.

Sniffing the pot was just a habit. Maybe he just wanted to know who'd been sniffing it when he'd been gone. Nordic had adopted the dog only a few months ago, saving him from the abuse of a demonic little boy who'd been teasing him with a stick, poking at him as though the no-good sprite were a troubadour, making the dog angry and scared. That one incident had light-ninged out from its source, causing a world of trouble for Nordic and Finn, whom he'd named after a tinker who used to frequent his family farm in Dakota and taught Anders how to make knives. He was an Irishman young Anders tolerated and counted among his closest friends. Leaving pile after pile of dead men in his wake, and a beautiful, beguiling young woman who'd helped Nordic and Finn fend off the horde of gun-hung ranchmen and townsmen and the notorious regulator, Gentleman Jim Ridgely, Nordic had left southern New Mexico, hearing that a rancher in Colorado needed someone to man a remote mountain line shack for the summer and winter…

Thus, here Nordic and Finn were, enjoying the peace and quiet of yet another shack in another remote mountain valley, this one nearly a stone's throw from the southern border of Wyoming Territory.

Nordic was halfway across the creek when the distant crack of a rifle reached his ears. The echoes dwindled on the breeze rustling the pine and aspen boughs around him.

"Whoa. Whoa, boy!" Nordic said, pulling back on Apache's reins.

He peered at the pine-clad mountain rising in the south, the forest touched with the gold and salmon of the dwindling light. The gun report had come from beyond that ridge.

As he stared toward the ridge, the gun spoke again, the report echoing, the echoes dwindling as they vaulted skyward.

"Who in the hell..." Nordic muttered, stitching heavy brows over blue Nordic eyes.

No one was supposed to be on Deveraux Range. Everyone knew that, even market hunters, though Nordic had had to send a few packing in past weeks. Believing he might have more rustlers on his hands, he reined Apache back out of the creek. He glanced over his shoulder at Finn. The dog stood on the porch, gazing in the direction from which the report had come, tail arched.

"Come on, Finn! Let's check it out!"

The dog forwent the steps and leaped straight down to the ground fronting the cabin and ran across the creek, catching up to Nordic as the big man put Apache into a gallop. He rode around the shoulder of the slope fronting the cabin and the creek and out into the broader valley beyond. He followed an old cattle trail down the heart of the valley as the gun cracked again...again...and again.

A girl screamed.

Nordic followed the sounds into a canyon angling off to the west side of the valley, following an old trail that Deveraux's men had cut when wood cutting in the late summer and early fall. This was a remote canyon Nordic had investigated only once, a month ago. Finding nothing suspicious and given its remoteness as well as a vast range to patrol, he had not investigated it again since.

Obviously, however, someone was in it now.

The pistol shots sounded as though they came from one gun—a revolver of maybe .45 caliber. Nearly as loud as a .44 repeating rifle. The one-gun theory ruled out a gunfight. Was one of Garth Deveraux's men doing some target shooting?

He rode up and over a low divide, Finn running close beside him and Apache. Thirty feet down the divide, he reined up sharply and curveted Apache, gazing straight down the steep hill and into a broad valley backing up against a steep, fir- and pine-carpeted ridge. A creek ran through the valley and the grass around it was a deep, verdant green and at least stirrup high.

A hundred yards beyond Nordic, a Conestoga-style wagon with a white canvas cover stretched across hoops was parked at the base of the ridge. Out front of the wagon, a man in blue trousers and red flannel shirt was doing a bizarre dance while one of the six men sitting a horse before him shot at his feet, dust and splintering sage branches blowing up around him. Flanking the dancing man were two women, both on their knees, one holding her arms around the other. Near them, to their right, a young, towheaded boy in trousers, white shirt, suspenders, and black immigrant hat, yelled, "Papa! Oh, Papa! Why are they doing this? Why are they on our land, Papa?"

The man doing the shooting shot into the ground near the boy's feet and bellowed, "Shut up, urchin! Or you'll dance, too!"

The boy screamed and ran around the far side of the wagon.

"He's just a boy!" the woman kneeling with the smaller, younger one shouted at the shooter.

The shooter, whom Nordic recognized as Deveraux's foreman, Wayne Bitterman, threw his head back and laughed. The others laughed, too. Then Bitterman turned to the other men and said, "Boys, let's show these hoopleheads what happens to nesters on Deveraux Range!"

He and the five others dismounted. With his pistol butt, Bitterman punched the man who'd been dancing. The man grunted, stumbled backward, and dropped on his back. He lay still, limbs stretched out wide to either side of him. Then Bitterman and the other men approached the women slowly, threateningly, like stalking mountain lions.

The girl screamed and lowered her head and covered it with her arms. Nordic could see her trembling even from this distance.

The older woman, whom Nordic assumed was her mother, yelled, "*No!* You stop right there! You have no right. This is open range!" Anders heard his own old-world accent in her voice. She was of Scandinavian extraction, too.

"Oh, for the love of God!" Nordic heeled Apache into a hard run down the divide. "Come on, Finn!"

Giving an excited bark, the dog ran along behind and then beside him.

As he galloped, Nordic slipped his Winchester from his saddle boot and cocked it one-handed. The Deveraux men's horses saw him and scattered. Bitterman and his men swung around and reached for their sidearms.

Nordic blew up a sage branch and grass in front of Bitterman and the man quickly removed his gloved right hand from his gun handle.

"Stop right there, Deveraux, or the next one will be in your guts!"

The other men also removed their hands from their sidearms. Nordic reined in Apache ten feet away from them and the kneeling, bawling women. Finn stopped beside him, barked once then arched his tail, lifted his hackles, showed his teeth at the hard cases, and growled.

"Nordic!" Bitterman shouted. "What are these people doing squatting on Deveraux land? It's your job to keep them out!"

Keeping the men covered with his rifle, Nordic said a little sheepishly, "I didn't know they were here. This is remote country. I didn't think…" He shrugged. Then the girl, maybe twenty years old, a pretty, blue-eyed blonde, looked up at him. Her day dress bulged at her belly. She was carrying.

Bitterman said, "You should have known they were here. It's your job to scour Deveraux Range. We rode into this canyon from the west and smelled the smoke." He glanced toward the far side of the wagon where smoke rose in a lazy plume. Nordic had seen it earlier. Now he smelled the stench of roasting meat.

Beef.

Oh, no, he thought. *Don't tell me they were rustling, too.*

He looked at the pregnant girl again. She returned his look with an expression of desperate pleading. Begging for him to save her and her family from the savage range riders.

A man groaned. She and Nordic both turned to see the man who'd been dancing lift his head and shake it as though to clear the cobwebs. He was tall, lean and had longish silver hair and a long, silver mustache on his ruggedly handsome face. Like the girl, he had blue eyes. They owned a frightened, befuddled cast.

"Papa!" The girl rose, ran over to him, and dropped to her knees beside him. She cradled his head in her lap. "Oh, Papa, are...are you all right?" She brushed a thumb through the blood on his lower lip.

"Sarah," he said with a vague, distant air. "Darling Sarah..."

The older woman remained on the ground, kneeling, staring in shock at the hard-faced men before her.

Bitterman turned to the older man, who was likely in his late fifties, early sixties, then gave his mustached upper lip an ironic curl, and said, "Now, ain't that sweet?"

Nordic gave the man a hard, savage stare, which he was good at doing with his chiseled, old-world, Scandinavian features that bespoke a man who did not compromise. "Were you going to rape these women?" he asked the foreman. "Kill the old man and the boy?"

"They're nesting! They killed one of Deveraux's beeves!"

"Can't you see the girl's in the family way, you useless savage? She needs the sustenance. Besides, Deveraux has more than two thousand head. He's not going to miss one beef!"

"They'll take more," said one of the others—a short, brown-haired, brown-mustached half-Mexican. Pablo "El Cuchillo" Gutierrez. In addition to a Bisley .44 hanging low on his right thigh, gunslinger style, he wore three knives in sheaths on his shell belt. He spread his dark brown mustache in a cruel, chip-toothed smile. "Many more. It is the way of the nester."

With the brunt of Nordic's attention on El Cuchillo, "The Knife," Bitterman closed his hand over his Colt .45. He whipped it up out of its holster. He would have shot Nordic out of his saddle if Finn hadn't been faster than the foreman. Instantly, Finn was on the man, leaping up off the ground and closing his jaws around the man's gun wrist, jerking it down while growling savagely.

Bitterman screamed. The gun barked. The bullet drilled through the toe of the foreman's right boot, making dust rise from the well-worn leather. The foreman screamed and dropped the gun. "You shot me in the foot, you cur!"

Bitterman tried to kick Finn. Again, the dog was faster. He wrapped his jaws around the man's ankle. The foreman lost his balance, gave another indignant cry, and dropped to his butt, cursing.

"Damn dog! Damn mean, worthless cur. I'll kill you for that!"

Finn stood glaring at the man, showing his teeth, tail curled up over his back.

"With what?" Nordic said, giving his own mustached upper lip an ironic curl. "You seem to have lost your gun."

The other men closed their hands around the handles of their own holstered six-shooters.

Nordic trained the Yellowboy on them. "Think it through," he told them. "No one's dead…yet."

Still on his butt, the ragged hole in the toe of his right boot oozing blood, Bitterman again pointed an arm and an enraged, accusing finger at the line shack man. "You work for Deveraux!" he screeched in exasperation. "That means you work for me!"

"I don't take orders from any rapist." Nordic hardened his voice and narrowed his blue eyes. "Now mount up—all of you. Get the hell out of here."

"Help me up!" Bitterman yelled at the half-Mex, who went over and helped his boss to his feet. He looked at Nordic. "Deveraux's gonna hear about this."

"Well, if he didn't, he'd likely wonder what had caused that hole in your boot." Again, the man from Dakota curled a grin. "Damn, I bet that hurts!"

Bitterman cursed, stepped forward tenderly, and began to reach for his Colt.

Finn took two steps toward him, growling a stern warning.

Bitterman looked at Nordic. "I want to pick up my gun!"

"Do it slow or you'll be missing a hand along with a toe." To the dog, Nordic said, "Easy, Finn."

The dog took one step backward but kept his angry glare on the foreman. Bitterman picked up the gun, watching the snarling dog closely. He slid the Colt into its holster and snapped the keeper thong into place over the hammer. To the other men, he barked, "Fetch my horse!"

When they'd walked off to fetch the foreman's horse as well as their own, Bitterman said, glancing at the pilgrims, "You get rid of these people. It's your job. Deveraux will likely fire you for not doing your job in the first place"—he looked down at the bloody hole in his boot—"as well as for this." He glared at Finn then turned to Nordic again. "But you get rid of them, or we'll be back…with more riders. And they'll *hang*!"

Nordic narrowed an eye in warning at the man, whose face was swollen and red in anger. "If you come back, I don't care how many you have with you, you'll wish you hadn't." He looked at the men returning, one mounted rider leading the foreman's black-and-white pinto. "Mount up and get the hell out of here."

When they'd ridden off to the west and the thuds of their horses' galloping hooves dwindled quickly,

Nordic turned to where the woman, the girl, and the man now stood side by side, near where Bitterman had punched the man down. There was still no sign of the boy.

"Who are you people?"

The man cleared his throat but still said raspily, in the lilting accent of the true Scandinavian, "We are the Iver Nordstrom family. This is my wife Hildegard, my daughter Sarah. The boy is Knut."

"From Dakota?"

"I'm originally from Sweden. My wife's family is from Norway. I married her in Bismarck, and we farmed with Sarah and Knut on our homestead until the drought came." He glanced at his pregnant daughter, who had her arms wrapped around her bulging belly. "And there was other trouble." His eyes were sad as he added, "We came out here because we heard the Colorado Rockies resembled my Swedish homeland. We wanted to start a new and better life together. The four of us." Again, he glanced at the girl. "The five of us."

"You can't do it here." Nordic slid his Yellowboy into its scabbard. "You'd best pull out first thing in the morning. They will be back."

"This is open range," Hildegard Nordstrom said tightly, her gray eyes cold, her jaws hard. She was a pretty woman somewhere in her forties, Nordic thought. She'd obviously passed on her looks to her pregnant young daughter.

Nordic shook his head. "Doesn't matter." He

reined Apache around and began to ride away. He stopped when Sarah asked, "Who are you, mister?"

Nordic glanced back at her. "Name's Nordic. Anders Nordic."

"You from Dakota?"

"Yes, ma'am." He glanced at the dog. "This is Finn." He pinched his hat to the Honyockers. "Good day."

He touched heels to Apache's flanks and he and Finn headed back in the direction from which they'd come…and had run into so much trouble.

It wasn't like Anders Nordic was any stranger to trouble, but this was big, sad trouble, indeed. He'd just kicked a nice Nordic family—practically his own people—with a pregnant daughter off land they had every right to be on.

What kind of man did that?

CHAPTER FOUR

Nordic was halfway back to his cabin when what he instinctively and immediately recognized as a bullet warbled through the air inches off his right ear to plunk into a tree behind and to his left.

Apache gave a shrill neigh and reared.

This wasn't Anders Nordic's first rodeo. He'd been shot at so many times in the past, it was almost old hat to him. He got the horse under tight rein and, while Finn barked angrily back in the direction from which the thundering report just now come on the heels of the bullet, Anders shucked his Yellowboy from its boot, swung his right leg over the horn, and dropped straight down to the ground. He slapped the Appaloosa's right hip.

"Go, boy! Get outta here!"

Another bullet slammed into the ground two feet to Anders's right, between him and Finn, who was running toward him. Finn yelped, jumped, twisted in the air, and landed on all fours growling and snarling.

As the bullet's whipping report reached Nordic's ears, he leaped and twisted just as the dog had done, and threw himself into a pine and fir forest that had been on his right before the first bullet had come.

"Come on, Finn!" he shouted just before he struck the ground on his hip and right shoulder.

The dog barked. Nordic could hear the rataplan of his racing paws just before he realized he'd thrown himself onto the side of a steep, needle-carpeted slope. He dropped the rifle and tried to gain purchase with his boot toes and fingertips, but the slope's downward angle was too severe. Gravity was not in his favor. His *sombrero* tumbled off his head as he gave a loud, "Ohhh...*noooo*!"

He rolled as though he'd been tossed by a muscular giant into a deep abyss. He rolled...and rolled...and rolled. To his right as he rolled, he glimpsed in a blur of quick motion the black-and-white collie dog rolling along beside him—the loyal dog close by his side even as he rolled likely to his own demise. He bounced off one pine, fir, and aspen after another, his body aching in every joint, bone, muscle, and sinew as he continued rolling...rolling... rolling.

He grunted and groaned.

Finn yelped, yipped, and whined as the poor dog, too, was battered by the trees around him.

Suddenly the ground beneath Nordic's battered body disappeared.

He dropped through thin air to be stopped suddenly by flat ground. He heard a great *whush* of displaced air and realized he'd made the sound himself as the ground blasted the air out of his lungs. Lying on his back, he saw Finn roll off the lip of the ravine and strike the ground ten feet away from Anders with a great grunt and a cry as the dog's own wind was punched out of him.

Finn lay on his side, whining and snarling at the same time, snapping his jaws as though at some unseen opponent.

Nordic lifted an aching arm to sweep his long, thick blond hair out of his bearded face, clarifying his vision so that he found himself looking up at the crowns of pines and spruces jutting toward a sky that was darkening to the deep green of an imminent sunset. He and the dog lay breathing heavily, chests and bellies expanding and contracting almost violently.

As Nordic lay there, only half conscious, assessing his condition—for full consciousness lay miles away —he was sure that nearly every bone in his body had been pummeled to chalk dust. As he did, there was a quiet thudding beside him. He turned his head to see his *sombrero* lying on the floor of the ravine between him and Finn.

For some reason, the hat amused him, lying there.

"Least," he said between labored breaths, "least-ways…I…got…my…topper…!"

He couldn't help laughing at that. It was short-lived mirth, for the laughter made his broken limbs grind their sharp, shattered edges together.

"*Ohhh!*" he groaned and rolled onto his side, drawing his knees toward his chest.

He lay there, breathing, aching, his ears ringing in agony, believing he'd moved his last when he heard a crying sound and then felt a cold nose in his left ear, sniffing. He looked up to see Finn standing over him, staring concernedly down at him, brown eyes cast with worry. The dog tilted his head from side to side then brushed at Nordic's left shoulder once…twice…three times with his right front paw.

"What?" the man grunted. "You still…alive? Me— I thought I was dead!"

The dog gave a plaintive wail and clawed two more quick times at Nordic's left shoulder with his right front paw.

"Don't you have nothin' broke?" Anders asked the dog. "Me—I don't think there's anything that *ain't* broke!"

What a day…

The dog moaned then turned and lifted his head to stare up the ridge down which they'd both rolled like rocks in a gravel slide…the toys of unkind gravity. Then Anders heard what the dog heard—men's voices and the crunch of gravel under boots.

"Oh, hell—they're comin' for us, are they?" Anders sat up and shook his head to try to clear his vision, which he only half accomplished. It was still partly blurry and the world of the sandy-floored ravine and the forest rising on his right slowly took shape.

He knew who the approaching men were. It didn't take a genius to know that Wayne Bitterman, despite one sore foot minus one toe, and his four men had been waiting for him to head back to the line shack he occupied to spring a bushwhack on Anders. He looked up the steep slope down which he and the dog had fallen. He saw the distant, shadowy figures of three men moving slowly, carefully down the ridge, weaving between the trees, grabbing branches so the merciless gravity that had wreaked havoc on Nordic and Finn did not assault them, too, like ragged dolls being abused by a lunatic child.

"Oh lordy," Nordic said, trying to heave himself to his feet, "not sure I can make it, Finn. You might have to leave this bag of useless bones here an' save yourself."

Finn moaned and licked his best friend's face.

"All right…I'm gonna try…"

He'd be damned if he didn't manage, after several stillborn attempts, to heave himself to his feet. He'd be damned, as well, despite all the aches and pains, if every bone, muscle, and sinew felt as though it were in its rightful place. He ached like hell, but one of the men now roughly halfway up the slope on his right stopped against a tree for balance, pointed around the tree toward the now-standing Anders, and yelled, "There!"

If Anders didn't feel a fresh spurt of anxious energy…

He reached for his bone-gripped .44 and was relieved to find it still in its holster. God looked after fools. He shucked the big popper, crouched, and fired three quick rounds up the slope, slowing each of his three assailants while wondering where the other two were. Then he shuffled to his left, up the shallow bank on that side, and into the forest beyond. The terrain sloped downward here, too, but nothing like the one that had pummeled him and Finn so mercilessly.

He ran in a shuffling, tender gait. Finn wasn't as fast as he normally was, either, but they made relatively good time in getting ahead of their attackers.

Guns hammered behind them, but their stalkers were still descending the steep slope, and their aims were less than true. As he and Finn ran, Nordic felt himself loosening up a little, so he was able to increase his speed albeit gradually. As he ran, the dog close beside him like always, Anders kept a cautious look around and ahead of him, wondering if the other two men with Bitterman had worked around him or to either side. He kept his pistol cocked and gripped tightly in his right fist, ready to shoot if needed.

The pops behind him and Finn grew gradually louder until the bullets began plunking into the trees around them and into the forest duff near their heels.

That told him he probably wasn't running as fast as he'd thought he was. His attackers were closing the gap between them and their quarry.

Nordic stopped abruptly and snapped off the rest of the loads in his Colt, sending all three men to cover.

He whipped around and continued running, yelling, "Come on, Finn. We're gonna have to hole up, too!"

They ran another hundred yards, the forest darkening quickly around them. In this case, he welcomed the coming night. They wouldn't be able to track him and the dog in the darkness.

Ahead and to either side several stone outcroppings humped up. Nordic aimed for one fifty yards ahead and on his right. It was the largest of the three others he saw.

Finn followed him around the backside of the stony dike, and right away Anders saw an alcove of sorts cut into the rock. He ducked into it, the dog close on his heels. It was roughly ten feet deep, a winding, dark corridor in the formation.

Nordic stopped and gave his back to the stony wall. A bulge in the rock hid him and the dog from the entrance, which was now a shadowy, jagged outline. The sun must have set, for the forest beyond the entrance was in a foggy twilight.

Exhausted and sore, the pain needling him again now that he'd stopped running in adrenaline-fueled desperation, he slid down the dimpled rock wall to his butt. Finn stared at him wonderingly, tilting his head this way and that.

"Sit, boy," Nordic said, running his left hand through the dog's thick fur at the back of his neck. "Take a load off."

The dog whined and sat, curling his shaggy tail around him.

"Good boy, good boy."

Nordic drew a deep breath against his needling aches and blew it out raggedly. "I think we're in the clear. Leastways, for now. If they'd seen this cavern, they'd be here by now. Likely still lookin' for us. If they come in to pull us out, they'll get pills they can't digest for their trouble."

He was reloading his empty Colt, ejecting the spent cartridges and replacing them with fresh ones his cartridge belt. He chuckled.

"Don't I sound confident, though? I'm a damn fool for letting us get bushwhacked like that, for not expecting a play by that snake Bitterman."

He chuckled again as he filled the last empty chamber in the Colt's wheel and closed the loading gate. "Leastways, I got my confidence. The confidence of a fool, but confidence just the same!"

He spun the cylinder and held the heavy Colt down between his legs.

Finn continued to stare at him, head cocked to one side, his floppy ears raised as far as he could raise them, which wasn't far.

"I know what you're thinkin' about, boy. Don't think I don't."

Finn turned his head to the other side and gave an incredulous, deep-throated moan of inquiry.

"You're thinkin' it's past your suppertime." Nordic chuckled.

He had to admit he'd worked up a powerful hunger himself.

First things first.

He and Finn waited in silence against the outcropping's rock wall.

What little light remained faded quickly until they sat in indigo darkness.

The air cooled. It grew right cold, in fact, this high in the Never Summers.

They'd been in the niche for a good ninety minutes when the heavy silence of the mountain night was broken by what sounded like the snap of a twig under a stealthy foot.

Presently, footsteps crunching pine needles grew louder.

Suddenly, they stopped.

Nordic rose slowly, wincing against the pain in his knees and hips.

He edged a look around the thumb in the rock wall to his right.

Starlight showed the silhouette of a man standing in the cavern's doorway. The weak light winked off the breech of the rifle in the man's two hands holding the long gun up high across his chest.

"Yoo-hoo," the man said softly, with jeering menace. "Anyone in here?"

Nordic said nothing. He glanced at Finn behind and gestured for the dog to remain quiet.

Anders edged another peek around the bulge in the rock wall.

The man's shadow turned. He sighed. Apparently, he wasn't sure the cavern was empty, but he lacked the spleen to check it out personally.

Nordic gestured for the dog to stay.

He holstered his pistol, shucked his big Green River knife he made from the sheath on his left hip, and hurried out from behind the bulge in the wall to the man now standing with his back to the entrance.

Anders raised the knife high and slammed the end of the handle down hard against the back of the man's head.

The man fell forward and struck the ground with a grunt.

Anders kicked him onto his belly, crouched over him, and slid the Green River's savagely upward-curved point against the tender skin beneath the man's chin.

"Ready to die, fella?"

He frowned, puzzled. There was enough of a moon that he could make out the man's face. There was at least enough light for him to realize this man had not been one of the five he'd encountered earlier at the Nordstrom family's camp.

"Who the hell are you?"

The man hardened his jaws and cast his ugly features in pure, jeering belligerence. "Wouldn't you just love to know?"

"All I do know," Anders said tightly through gritted teeth, "is you came gunnin' for the wrong man an' dog, fella."

He drove the blade hilt deep in the man's neck.

Finn came running out of the cavern and sniffed the bleeding, dying man, whining his own incredulity.

Anders pulled the knife out of the man's neck and cleaned it on the still-quivering man's shirt. He retrieved his rifle, said, "Come on, Finn!"

Man and dog lit out into the darkness beyond the cavern.

CHAPTER FIVE

Alexandra Deveraux stared out the window of her private carriage and across the broad, flat, grassy, sage-carpeted floor of the Kawuneeche Valley in the heart of the Never Summer Mountains, where she'd been born twenty-four years ago and raised on her family's vast holdings at the top of Comanche Mountain.

Warmth filled her.

It wasn't only the high-altitude sunshine pouring in the coach's window that so warmed her. It was the primitive warmth of returning to her home as well as to her roots, to a rush of memories that, one by one and two by two, comprised her young life.

The carriage carried her along the twisting, turning Avalanche Creek, south of Poudre Canyon and the Cache la Poudre River, reminding her of when she and her brothers had fished and swam here at least three times a week every summer, somehow finding ways to escape their regiment of daily chores at the ranch headquarters. Billy, Brian, and Alexandra had picked berries along these rippling, soothing waters, as well, eating nearly as many as they'd picked to be mildly chastised by their mother, Louise, upon returning home with maybe one bucket for the five hours they'd been out there, picking and swimming.

The carriage suddenly swung off the main trail to follow the secondary trail that would take her up Comanche Mountain to her family's ranch headquarters that sat on the broad, relatively flat top of the hogback mountain, near Cameron Pass and just south of the awe-inspiring formation known as the Crags. The ranch headquarters was ensconced in Douglas firs, ponderosa pines, and Engelmann spruce, all of which jutted high above the sprawling main lodge so that they seemed to be tickling the underbelly of the vaulting, cobalt sky.

The carriage rocked on its thoroughbraces as it made its way up the switchbacking trail, the aromatic conifers pushing up close along the trace.

The carriage was, in fact, a reoutfitted Conestoga her father had purchased especially to take Alexandra to and from the train station in Denver when she'd started attending the Seabury Private Academy in New York City and then had stayed on after graduating with honors to teach courses in Greek and European literature.

He'd had the carriage repainted, its brass fittings polished till they shone, and the seats freshly upholstered in cowhide. There was even an eating tray that Alexandra could pull out from under the rear seat so

that she could dine in relative comfort on the ham
sandwiches, pickled eggs, pickled cucumbers, and
cheese wheels her mother had always supplied her
with on each trail to Union Station in the burgeoning
cow town of Denver.

Her father had even supplied her, unbeknown to
Alexandra's mother, with French champagne in a
bucket of ice chipped from the block in their own ice
shed behind the Comanche Mountain headquarter's
main lodge.

Alexandra smiled, thinking of her father's and
mother's doting.

"Alexandra," she gently admonished herself now,
"you are one spoiled girl."

She chuckled.

Her father was a tough old buffalo with an English
accent that didn't fit his bullish bearing, but while he
was strict, he'd coddled her just the same.

One more broad turn along the edge of a canyon
from which the conifers jutted dramatically. Then the
canyon slid away to the left of the trail. There was a
straight stretch of trail and then the pines pulled away
on both sides. Alexandra's heart quickened. She knew
every tree along the trail, every twist and turn, every
rock and boulder, so that she was never in doubt when
she was almost home. Now the trees fell back and the
trail ahead broadened into the Comanche Ranch's yard
with the lodge on a rise to the left and the bunkhouse,
barns, stables, corrals, and other outbuildings on the
right.

Her heart rose with delight, nearly taking her breath away.

As always, cowboys sat on the rails of the circular breaking corral, watching one rider break a wild, wide-eyed bronc, its rich mane glinting in the sunshine on the ranch that had been named by Alexandra's grandfather. Kinsley Deveraux had been killed by rustlers only two years after Alexandra had been born. As always, all the hands—there were seven out there now —turned to watch the carriage roll into the yard, expressions of delight on their faces. They all removed their hats, a couple jeeringly elbowing the others.

The bronc rider got distracted by the young lady's return and was thrown violently off the bronc's left hip to land in a pile of dust wafting around him. The hands were aware of the "Princess of the Comanches" return, of course. Word spread fast even if her father and mother tried to keep it a secret. Such returns usually caused a great stir, and on such nights the hands would sit up late in their bunkhouse drinking, gambling, laughing, arguing, and dancing to a fiddle, though Alexandra herself was allowed nowhere near that raucous crowd.

As the coach rocked to a stop, Alexandra regarded the bronc buster who'd been thrown violently off the bronc's left hip to land so unceremoniously, dust wafting around him.

Alexandra winced and nibbled a thumbnail. "Oh, dear…"

"Young lady, get out here at once," came a deep, English accented voice from the lodge side of the coach as Alexandra studied the bronc rider, slowly, achingly climbing to his feet with the help of one other. "You have your father's cheek to kiss, missy!"

Alexandra smiled instantly, her concern for the bronc buster quickly vanishing, and turned to stare out the window on the opposite side of the coach.

Her father stood there, broad, tall, and handsome in his checked shirt, doeskin vest, and high-crowned, crisp black Stetson banded with a rattlesnake skin. At sixty-three, Garth Deveraux was still a handsome man, though Alexandra could see his face was craggier and vaguely more hollow-cheeked than the last time she'd seen him. He was so tanned he appeared half-Indian.

Her mother's long illness and death had taken some life out of him, as well. His gray eyes weren't as clear as before—they'd lost some of the old Deveraux brashness, confidence, and luster. His gray brows seemed more pronounced, as though to conceal the sadness in his eyes. His face appeared narrower, more lined, and it had lost some of its usual deep bronze.

Suddenly, Alexandra's delight in her homecoming was tempered by the fact of her mother's recent death. She smiled with affection at her father but also choked back a sob as Garth Deveraux opened the coach door and extended his hand to her, smiling and chuckling, while Riley Otis, the Deveraux coach driver who also assisted the ranch house's butler, set a small portable step on the ground before the door.

"Thanks, Riley," Alexandra said.

"Mmm, of course, Miss Deveraux." He bowed as though she were a member of the royal family then, knowing her father didn't like the men fawning over her, hurried away.

Despite the confining traveling frock and picture hat she wore, she hurried out of the coach to be engulfed in her father's strong arms, pressing her right cheek against his broad chest, relieved to hear the strong beat of his heart, which had taken such emotional abuse in the long year of his wife's passing from bone cancer.

Alexandra Deveraux took a deep sniff of the man —she'd always loved his unique, masculine tang of sage, whisky, and tobacco. She closed her eyes and patted his chest, for a few fleeting seconds imagining she was two-year-old Alex again, climbing onto her father's lap while he sat by the great room hearth in his bull-horn chair, enjoying French brandy and a good cigar.

When times were hard, she always brought the warmth and comfort of that time to her mind. It had never failed to settle her down. It did now, as well, tempering a little the fresh sorrow of her mother's passing. The feeling was fleeting, however, shoved away by a lingering acrimony.

She reached up and sandwiched her hands clad in white traveling gloves around his broad, craggy, clean-shaven face. "Father, you awful, awful man. You lout! Why on earth did you not tell me earlier that Mother's condition had worsened? I'd have traveled straight-away and helped you with her." Tears dampened her eyes, and she choked back another sob. "I could have spent time with her—her last days!"

A man's voice sounded behind her. "Pardon me, Miss Devereaux. Just wanted to welcome you back and ask if I can help with your luggage."

Alexandra turned to see a young, tall, slender blond man standing at the coach's rear corner, his hat in his hands, an unctuous smile on his hatchet face.

Before Alexandra could say anything, her father said commandingly and with raw disdain, "Mr. Otis can handle it just fine, O'Brien. Push on, now! Can't you see I'm welcoming my daughter home?"

O'Brien's lower jaw sagged. His eyes were stunned, and a humiliated flush rose in his cheeks. His lips moved but he didn't say anything.

"Go over to the bunkhouse and see if the doc needs help with Bitterman," Garth Deveraux ordered.

"Go on, go on—git!" said Riley Otis, turning the young man around and giving him a kick in the pants. Otis was a large Black man nearly as old as Deveraux, but he was still nimble and strong. Also, a good game hunter, he provided a lot of food for the Deveraux kitchen. He'd already brought a wheelbarrow over and was starting to load it with the many pieces of luggage in the coach's boot.

Looking even more shocked and indignant than before, O'Brien staggered away, his face as red as a Colorado sunset, stuffing his hat down on his head. Over at the breaking corral, the other hands were laughing. They had either goaded O'Brien into coming over here or they'd paid him to do it for entertainment and to see how their boss, the uncompromising Garth Deveraux, would react. Even in their twenties, men were boys. Even in their thirties. She'd never had a good experience with a single one.

"Sorry about that, Miss Deveraux. I gotta pay closer attention," said Riley Otis, grunting as he planted a large steamer trunk into the wheelbarrow then began pushing it toward the big main lodge with a grunt.

"It's not your fault, Riley," Alexandra said. "Thank you, though."

When the big man had left, Devereaux said, "Sorry, honey. I'll keep them away from you—don't you worry. Now that you're moving back full time, it's going to be a chore, but I have a two-barrel greener leaning against the wall by the front door."

He winked and smiled.

It was true. Alexandra was moving back to the Comanche Ranch. She'd loved teaching but she'd had her fill of the city and the Eastern life in general. Her mother's death had made her especially homesick. Part of her felt that by moving back, she'd be close to her mother's spirit.

She gave her father a castigating look, narrowing one eye. "Don't think our topic of conversation can be so easily changed, Father."

Deveraux groaned, wagged his head, and sighed. "You sure have your mother's spirit, young lady. Can we at least repair to the parlor for brandies, so I can steel myself against the Deveraux lady castigation?"

"Indeed," Alexandra said, brightening. "I could use something to cut the trail dust."

Deveraux stuck out his elbow. "Shall we?"

Alexandra hooked her arm through it. "We shall."

As they started up the cinder-paved trail toward the main lodge, a man's shrill scream issued from the bunkhouse to the right of the breaking corral. "Consarn it, Doc—will you quit your foolin' an' just cut the damn thing *off*?!"

Alexandra glanced up at her father, brows stitched. "Was that Bitterman, Father? What's going on?"

Deveraux sighed as they continued walking. "There's been trouble, honey. Big trouble involving a big man from Dakota occupying one of my line shacks." He sighed again, shook his head. "It'll blow over, I'm sure."

"Probably not if Wayne Bitterman is involved."

"No, probably not."

CHAPTER SIX

Like most Westerners, Anders Nordic wasn't accustomed to walking.

He rarely walked much farther than to the privy flanking his cabin and stable.

That's why his feet burned and ached as though he were treading over glowing hot coals by the time he was halfway back to his cabin. He winced with every step. He'd whistled for his Appaloosa, as Apache usually came to his whistle, but Nordic had a feeling the stallion had run all the way back to the shack, which he judged he'd been roughly six miles from when he and Finn had been ambushed.

Finn by his side as always, except to chase the night sound of some burrowing creature now and then, Nordic kept walking, steering by the stars and the mountains silhouetted against the sky around him. This was wild, crazy country, and most men who hadn't lived here all their lives would likely get quickly lost, trying to make their way back to their cabin at night from six miles away.

But Nordic, who'd spent many years in the mountains, and despite his having grown up on the rolling Dakota prairie, had learned to take note of every rock, tree, and formation he came upon during his travels. He also knew the stars in the night sky. By using these skills as well as having a good, calm sense of direction, he'd never gotten lost for more than a few minutes at a time.

This night, he was momentarily disoriented when he'd found himself heading up the wrong canyon but got his bearings back quickly and then, just as quickly, he saw below him the stream meandering through the ravine fronting his shack, the shack itself showing like a pale shadow in the light of the quickly sagging moon on the stream's other side.

He stopped when hoof thuds sounded.

He dropped to a knee, raising the Yellowboy, ready to rack a live cartridge into the chamber. He stayed the action when Finn gave a low moan and wagged his tail.

The dog didn't sense a threat, which soothed Anders's nerves. Then he saw why the dog sensed no threat. In the woods to his left, a moving shadow gathered shape before him, becoming a horse, and the moonlight brushed across the Appaloosa stopping before Nordic and the dog, who mewled happily, delighted to see his friend.

The Appaloosa lowered his head and pawed the ground, then lifted his head and shook it.

Nordic rose, grabbed the mount's reins, whispered, "Come on, Finn," and led the horse back up the low, wooded hill down which he and the dog had walked. "I do believe Apache is tellin' us we got trouble!"

Anders led the horse and the dog up and over the crest of the low ridge. Twenty feet down from the crest, he stopped in a cluster of rocks and turned to Apache who regarded him wide-eyed.

Nordic knew the horse as well as he knew the dog, and he could see the enervation in Apache's eyes just as he could sense it in the heavy way the horse was breathing. He ran a soothing hand down the horse's long, fine snout and said, "Easy, boy. Easy, fella. Everything's all right." He studied the horse staring apprehensively back at him. "But it's not, is it? That's what you're tryin' to tell me."

The horse whickered, stomped one front foot, shook his head.

Finn sat nearby, cocking his head from side to side, studying the Appaloosa. The dog knew, too, that Apache was upset about something.

Again, Nordic ran his hand down the horse's snout, soothing him.

He looked around cautiously, wondering if Apache was trying to alert him about an ambush. Or was someone in the cabin, waiting for him?

Something told him the latter scenario was the most likely. The cabin door had no lock on it. Bushwhackers could easily get in. From inside, they'd have an easier time bushwhacking the man they might be expecting—namely, the man they'd tried to ambush six miles to the southwest and where they'd left one man in case Nordic had remained in that canyon.

Which he had…until he'd killed that man.

Meanwhile, the others had gone on to the cabin to wait for him.

He nodded. Yes, that had to be how it was.

He hunkered on his haunches, pulled pensively at the long, green grass.

How to play it?

Why should *he* play it? Let *them* play it. After all, they're *here* to play it.

He unsaddled Apache, tossed the gear on the ground. He produced his spyglass from his saddlebags then dropped the bags to the ground, as well.

"We're gonna wait 'em out, boy."

He moved up to the crest of the ridge, raised the glass, and gazed down through the gauzy darkness toward the cabin down the opposite slope and to the slight rise beyond the stream.

He couldn't see anything yet. But judging by how the moon was quickly dropping in the west and how the stars were slowly fading, he would soon.

———

With the dog sitting beside him, the Appaloosa standing a few feet down the slope behind him in a state of sleepless agitation, Nordic waited.

He felt himself doze off a time or two then admonished himself to stay alert.

Obviously, trouble was afoot or Apache wouldn't

have acted as he had. He wasn't sure the trouble would come from the cabin. He just had a feeling. But it could come from anywhere. That's why he off-cocked the Yellowboy's hammer and set it down close beside him, on his right side. On his left, Finn dozed with his chin on his crossed paws, snoring softly.

Nordic kept a close eye on the slope behind him, on the wooded ridge around him, on the wooded slope dropping away below him, toward the creek.

No movement except the rustle of grass and the faint scratching of branches in a vagrant breeze.

The only sounds were the occasional screech of nightbirds including the tooth-gnashing one of an owl catching a rabbit and the baby-like screaming that followed. Between such sounds, silence.

The stars continued to fade.

A pale wash grew between and behind the toothy eastern ridges, out on the prairie beyond the little settlement of Camp Collins and the army fort that sat along the Cache la Poudre River.

The true dawn grew. The darkness faded so that Anders could see the cabin—a gray-brown splotch on the bank on the other side of the stream. It became clearer as the sun rose and then, when the sun was halfway above the eastern horizon, the cabin door opened. Two men stepped out, one behind the other. They looked around cautiously, holding their rifles straight out before them, tracking them, looking for a target they seemed sure they'd find.

Yep, they'd been expecting Nordic, all right.

He hooked a crooked, cunning smile. He'd disappointed them. Here, he'd had no company for months and he hadn't been here to enjoy them. He chuckled silently at that. No one wanted to be farther away from people than Anders Nordic did. He'd always been that way. From a very early age.

Sitting beside him, Finn stared down the ridge through the trees. He glanced at Anders and gave a questioning little mewl.

"I got no reason why they'd want to kill me, Finn. Maybe they're rustlers. Maybe someone's put a price on my head. I wouldn't doubt it. I've killed enough men during my time in the West." He gave his blond-bearded head a slow wag. "Not a one of them that didn't need it, though."

The interlopers disappeared around the backside of the cabin.

They reappeared fifteen minutes later, riding up along the cabin's right wall, fully mounted. One was small, one large. The larger man wore a bowler hat and he had a thick, black mustache. The small man wore a low-crowned, flat-brimmed cream Stetson. He wore a brindle beard, and he had two pistols tied low on his thighs, gunslinger style. He wore a broadcloth coat over a white shirt. On the outside, he wore a bear fur coat against the morning chill. The bigger man wore a poncho of coyote fur.

They each rode with their rifles butt down on their right thighs, barrels aimed skyward.

As they started across the stream, looking around cautiously, Nordic said, "Here they come, boy. Let's get back." He smiled as he crawled straight down the slope from the ridge. "Give 'em the surprise of their lives."

He stood and walked over to Apache, who regarded him apprehensively. "'Pache," he said, wrapping his gloved hands around the Appaloosa's snout, "time to be really quiet, all right? No whickers, no neighs, no hoof stomps, no head shakes, no tail switches—nothin'. You got that, boy?"

The horse just stared at him, but Nordic knew the horse well enough to know that he'd gotten it.

"All right, then."

Anders released Apache's snout and regained his position just below the crest of the ridge. The dog retook his place beside him, tail curled around him. Anders could hear the slow clomps of approaching hooves.

Nordic glanced at Finn. "That goes for you, too," he whispered.

The dog looked at him, slightly twitching one ear, shifted his weight from one front foot to the other, then turned his head back forward to stare up at the ridge crest before him.

As the hoof thuds, crackle of pine needles, and crunch of old leaves grew gradually louder on the other side of the rise, Nordic slowly picked up his Winchester, clicked the hammer back to full cock, and held it on the ground before him, absently caressing the hammer with his thumb. He lifted his head to stare higher on the rise. A few seconds later, the crowns of the two men's hats came into view. They were nearly to the ridge crest.

Nordic let both horses take one more step and then he rose to his knees and then to his full height and raised the cocked Yellowboy's stock to his right shoulder, narrowing one eye as he aimed down the barrel at the two men.

He said with quiet menace, "What makes you two think you can feel so free with my cabin?"

Seeing him, seeing the Winchester aimed at them, both men's eyes grew round as saucers. They jerked back on their reins and their horses' heads came up hard, eyes even wider than those of their riders. Wide and white-ringed. The big man reached for the rifle protruding from the saddle boot strapped to the right side of his saddle.

Anders shot him. The man yelped and flew back off the left side of his gray.

The other man raised his own rifle.

Nordic cocked the Winchester, ejecting the spent cartridge, and shot him, too. He grunted as the bullet plundered his brisket. He went flying ass over teakettle over the arched tail of his startled grullo. Both horses swung around hard, buck-kicked, and ran back down the ridge up which they'd just come.

Nordic racked another round into the Winchester's chamber, off-cocked the hammer, and let the rifle hang straight down along his right leg. He stared down at the two men who lay unmoving before him.

Dead.

Dammit.

He'd wanted to keep at least one of them alive so

he could find out who they were and what they wanted, but he'd botched it.

"Not gonna find out this way," he admonished himself as Finn ran up to each man, sniffing them, making water on the big man's right boot. He kicked his back feet, arching his back and his tail, then walked up to Nordic and sat down beside him.

"You're too much, Finn," Nordic said with a chuckle. "You're too much. You're in good company that way. I am, too."

He looked at the dead men again, considered his options.

Then he set his rifle down and moved down the slope, intending to run down the two men's horses. When given free rein, horses usually returned to their home barn. He hoped these two would, too. He'd follow them to see where they ended up. Maybe there, wherever "there" was, he'd find out who had a big enough beef with him to want him kicked out with a cold shovel, which he sensed was what they'd wanted.

Running down two horses after shooting their riders off was no picnic. With Finn's help, however, the dog hazing both mounts toward Anders who moved calmly, offering apples from his saddlebags, he managed to finally grab the reins of both.

He led them back to the top of the ridge, tied them to a pine branch, and slung each rider atop his horse, belly down. He tied them wrists to ankles beneath the horses' bellies and was nearly finished with the task when Finn, sitting nearby, barked loudly, angrily, warningly.

Turning to stare in the direction the dog was staring, Anders said, "What is it, bo—"

He stopped. Two riders were approaching from sixty yards away, trotting their mounts, heading up the slope on which Anders and Finn had waited for the two riders who'd trespassed on his cabin. Nordic squinted. One rider was his aging and uncompromising employer, Garth Deveraux.

The other rider was a young woman in a black poncho, long, lush, chestnut hair bouncing across her shoulders.

CHAPTER SEVEN

Finn continued to bark at the newcomers until Nordic said, "That's enough, boy. Come!"

The excited dog whined as he turned and ran over and sat down beside his master.

The two riders drew rein roughly ten feet from Nordic and Finn and cast their gazes over the dead men tied belly down across their saddles. Anders couldn't take his eyes off the young woman riding to the left of the man he knew was her father. The features—clean lined, evenly proportioned, and regal —were too familial than for it to be otherwise. They both radiated a haughty pride, even arrogance, though neither one had yet said anything.

They sat their saddles like they'd been born to them, with a light hand on the reins of their well-trained, blooded horses. The young woman wore a brown leather hat, and her long, chestnut hair continued to slide around behind her shoulders in the breeze. Her smooth, broad cheeks were touched with red from the sun, her mouth wide and full, her nose long and fine, her jaws hard and assured.

When she turned to Nordic, her cobalt eyes seemed to look right through him. He didn't like being stunned by anyone, but this girl's beauty stunned him, indeed.

She said nothing, only probed him with her gaze in a way that told him she already knew much about him, though they hadn't yet exchanged a single word.

Deveraux turned to him with his hard, gray-eyed gaze, the skin above the bridge of his broad, masculine nose wrinkling, gray brows stitching. "Rustlers?" With his accent, it came as *rustlas?*

"I don't know. They ambushed me yesterday six miles from here. There were three. The third one's dead. These two rode ahead, spent the night in my cabin. Aimed to give me a welcome home party in lead, I think."

"Let me see their faces," Deveraux said.

"What's that?"

"Let me see their faces."

Nordic glanced at the girl. She was no girl, however. She was young—mid-twenties, probably— but all the girlishness was gone. What was left was a beautiful, prideful, confident young woman owning as much of a sense of herself as her father did.

She returned his gaze with a cool one of her own. "I've seen dead men before, Mr. Nordic."

Anders glanced at Deveraux, who stretched his lips in a vague sort of prideful mirth.

Nordic walked over to the bigger of the two dead

men and drew his head up by a handful of hair, exposing his face.

Deveraux inspected the face, scowling, then shook his head.

"The other one," he said.

Anders let the big man's head drop back down against the barrel of his horse then walked over and showed Deveraux the other man's face.

Again, Deveraux shook his head. "I know most of the men around here, especially those with a propensity to steal other men's cattle. I don't recognize either of them. They might be after you alone, not me."

Nordic sighed.

"I'm Alexandra Deveraux," the woman said, leaning forward to extend a gloved hand to Nordic. She stretched her lips in a subtle smile much like the one her father had just shaped.

Anders glanced at Deveraux, who looked at him stonily. Anders moved a little stiffly forward to give the woman's hand a gentle shake. "Anders Nordic," he said, feeling a schoolboy flush rise in his cheeks.

Alexandra Deveraux gazed deeply, unabashedly into his eyes with those otherworldly, deep-blue ones of her own. He liked the feeling of her hand in his. Strong yet feminine. She gave his a shake.

When he stepped back, feeling self-conscious, still feeling his boss's stony gaze on him, Alexandra Deveraux said, "What's your dog's name?"

"That's Finn."

"Hello, Finn."

The dog moaned deep in his throat, switched his

weight from one foot to the other, glanced at Nordic, and gave a single, anguished bark. Anders wanted to laugh. He knew how the dog felt. Being in the presence of such rare beauty way out here made a man want to cut his own arm off with a rusty saw. He felt twelve years old again, a boy with a crush.

Anders glanced at Deveraux.

The man's hard expression told him silently but in no uncertain terms that his daughter was strictly off-limits. Nordic hadn't seen her before. But then he'd only visited the Comanche headquarters once, when he'd first been hired to ride out the year in the rancher's remote line shack. Something told Anders that she was either back from a long journey or that she'd been east to some fancy finishing school.

She was probably home for a visit. He sensed she'd missed these mountains, this rough country. She was as much a part of this wild country as her father.

If she was back visiting, he wondered how long she'd be here in the Never Summers. Not that it mattered. Her father's demeanor told him that this would likely be the only time he'd see her.

That was all right with Anders. He didn't like how this girl made him feel. He was a big man, but he felt small and boyish and inconsequential in her presence. Something told him he wasn't the only man she made feel that way. Something also told him that the men around the Comanche headquarters didn't get a whole lot of sleep when Miss Deveraux was around. Thinking about a woman like that could make a man mighty restless.

Deveraux said, "The doctor from Camp Collins removed my foreman Bitterman's toe yesterday. Or what was left of it."

"Sorry to hear that."

"No, you're not."

Nordic saw Alexandra Deveraux's cheeks flush a little. She seemed to fight off a smile. She looked down at her saddle horn, brushed a gloved thumb across it.

"Did they tell you how that happened, Mr. Deveraux?"

"They didn't need to. They are hard, uncompromising men. I don't say I approve of everything they do, but they get it done for me. Stay out of their business next time. And make sure those hoopleheads in Granite Valley are gone by tomorrow. No compromises. Understand?"

"The girl's in the family way."

Deveraux neck reined his horse around. "No compromises, Mr. Nordic. If I have to, I'll stretch hemp." He glanced at his daughter and said, "Come, Alexandra."

He booted his fine cream into a hard run back down the ridge up which they'd ridden. Alexandra Deveraux glanced at Nordic, dubiously, then reined her fine black around and galloped after her father. Nordic watched them go, the young woman's hair blowing back wildly in the wind.

Finn stared after them, moaning.

"You got me in trouble with the boss, Finn."

Finn glanced up at him, gave his tail a sheepish

wag, then turned his gaze to the dwindling riders and barked.

———

Anders untied the big man's horse from the tree and slapped its left hip. "Gid-yup, there, boy! *Gooo!*"

The horse galloped off down the slope up which the Deveraux father and daughter had just ridden. He did the same to the other man's horse. It gave a couple of buck-kicks as it rode away, whinnying, not at all appreciating having a dead man tied to its back.

"We'll see where they go," Anders told Finn. "I'm hoping they'll run back to where they came from. Then, maybe, I'll find out who sent those three hard-tails to turn me toe down."

Of course, it might have been those three alone who'd wanted him dead. But he didn't think so. He'd never seen them before. They might have been intent on avenging someone he'd killed—a rustler.

Recently, he'd killed many men in New Mexico around the little town of Cimarron when he'd saved the homeless Finn from a sadistic redheaded kid who'd been abusing him with a stick. The kid had turned out to be the son of the town's powerful banker, and that small, seemingly harmless incident had sparked off a chain of violent events the likes of which Nordic had never known before.

The likes of which he never would have thought possible until it had happened, and he'd found himself hunted in every nook and cranny of the Chama Mountains.

Usually, avengers didn't shoot a man from long-range.

They usually killed their avengers closeup, first making sure they knew why they were about to kill you.

Staring after the two galloping horses, Nordic shook his head.

No, those two and the first stalker Nordic had killed had been hired by someone else to kill him. Probably not for revenge but for some other reason Anders was dying to know.

No pun intended.

Anders saddled and bridled Apache and, a little bleary-eyed from lack of sleep, his feet still sore from the long walk back to the cabin, he, Finn, and Apache headed off down the ridge on the trail of the two horses. He didn't have much hope his plan would pan out, but all he could do was try. He had no other options by way of finding out who wanted him dead.

Of course, him being a contrary cuss who'd killed many men—none of whom hadn't deserved killing, however—and being seen as just generally unlikeable because of his gruff, taciturn manner and unwilling to take any guff from anyone, he wasn't unaccustomed to being targeted. But usually he knew *why* someone had wanted him turned toe down.

It was necessary to know who wanted him dead so all the advantages wouldn't be on their side of the table.

He followed the horses' tracks for a couple of miles until it became reasonably clear that they were headed in the direction of Camp Collins, a little settlement along the Cache la Poudre. They rode together, which was interesting. That meant they both had probably come from the same place. Nordic was both surprised and incredulous when he followed the two horses into Camp Collins then stopped on the main street angling through to see both mounts standing outside the Hans Becker Livery & Feed.

A small group of men were milling around the horses, conversing in fascination, crouching to see their faces. A stocky, jowly, bearded man in overalls—whom Nordic assumed was the livery barn owner—was at the center of the pack, looking even more red-faced with astonishment than the other onlooking townsmen. A man wearing a town marshal star was approaching the livery barn from up the street from Nordic, led by a young man in overalls and a black immigrant cap, probably a hostler from the livery barn who'd been sent to fetch the law.

Nordic booted Apache ahead, reining up near the crowd gathered around the dead men. He looked at the jowly, bearded gent and said, "Who in blazes are they?"

The bearded man looked at him. He didn't look happy. He had enough to do without having to deal with dead men riding in on his livery mounts. He threw out his arms, shrugging. "Got no idea. They an' another fella came in on the stage two days ago, rented these hosses, an' that's the last I seen of 'em…till now."

He turned his attention to the lawman pushing his way through the crowd, growling, "Out o' the way now! Out o' the way! Gimme room. Hans, what do we have here?"

"Don't ask me, Marshal," Hans said in exasperation. "I know those hosses, Li'l Boy an' Chub, but I don't know these *men*!"

Nordic cursed and reined Apache around. "Come on, Finn," he said. "Let's get the hell outta…"

His voice trailed off.

He'd just smelled the distinctive aroma of fermenting wort.

Beer.

It seemed to be coming from Lars Olson's Brewery & Saloon just up the street on his left—a long, low building he'd stopped in before for a beer, when he'd come to town for supplies.

Nordic loved beer. He usually brewed a rich, dark brown ale himself, but he hadn't been able to find a good source of hops in these parts. He couldn't grow it himself because he never stayed in one place long enough. He hadn't enjoyed a beer since his last trip to town, which was over a month ago. He hated towns more than almost anything else. No, he hated towns more than anything.

Still, he loved to belly up to a polished mahogany bar—or even rough pine planks—now and then and enjoy a cool, dark ale. He knew Olson's Brewery & Saloon offered just such fare. The only problem was,

Nordic had to make sure he was on his best behavior. Folks annoyed him. He had a short fuse. Nasty combination. That combination had landed him in a hoosegow here and there about the West more times than he wanted to think about.

He had to tread carefully, keep his head down, be inconspicuous, and not make trouble.

The inconspicuous part was especially hard as it would be hard for any man standing six and a half feet tall and with a gruff, bearded, muscular countenance. Just his physique alone sometimes attracted trouble. Men seemed to want to test themselves against him.

He looked down at Finn sitting on the street beside him, looking up at him apprehensively.

"Just one?" he beseeched the dog.

Finn, for whom this was not his first rodeo, showed his teeth and growled.

"Oh, hell—just one, Finn. Lighten up a little. A man needs a beer now an' then!"

Finn snorted, wagged his head, and gave a yip to show his dismay.

Nordic grinned and booted Apache over to the hitchrack fronting Lars Olson's Brewery & Saloon.

CHAPTER EIGHT

Olson's Saloon was busy now at noon, many men from the mountains and the surrounding ranches partaking hungrily of the free lunch counter that came with the purchase of a nickel beer.

Men milled about the room, talking loudly, joking and laughing. Most of the tables were occupied, and there were few gaps between the men standing at the bar eating ham, cheese, and pickled eggs from plates and nursing beers and throwing back shots of whisky.

There was a high hum of conversation.

Tobacco smoke hung heavy.

As Nordic made his way to the bar, he thought he heard the clack of toenails on the floor behind him. He turned and was surprised to see that Finn had followed him into the saloon. Anders raised a shaggy, blond brow. That was odd. When he'd entered a shop or saloon on one of his rare, previous visits to town, Finn had usually waited outside for him, and often at the edge of town. Finn hated towns as much as Nordic himself did, having had few good experiences among large congregations of men…and children.

"What's happening, fella?" Anders said.

Finn sat before him, looking sheepish.

Still frowning his curiosity, Nordic stepped around the dog to peer over the batwings. He realized right away what had driven the dog into the saloon with him. There were several young boys roughly the ages of the redheaded little rat who'd abused Finn with a stick that fateful day he and Nordic had fallen in together. One of those boys was carrying a stick, clubbing it against the posts of the telegraph line running along the far side of the street.

"I see, fella," Nordic said. "Stay close. We'll watch over each other."

He chuckled then found a gap in the men lined up at the bar. When one of the two busy aprons leaned over the counter toward him, turning one ear to him, Anders ordered an ale and small pan of beer for his dog.

The apron nodded, as such an order was not uncommon. Anders smiled at that. When the two beers came, he set the small pan down on the floor at the base of a ceiling support post, and Finn went to work on it, lapping.

Nordic turned back to the bar and began nursing his ale. The rich, malty brew was not easy to nurse, however, and in just a couple of minutes he'd emptied his glass. He glanced back at Finn, who'd finished his own beer and was sitting at the base of the post, tail curled around him, surveying the raucous crowd around him.

Guiltily, hoping Finn didn't notice, Anders beckoned for the bartender and ordered another beer. He found himself leaning over the bar and whispering into the man's ear, not wanting Finn to overhear. When the apron had nodded and headed off to the spigot poking up out of a big beer barrel, Nordic chuckled. He felt as guilty as a cheating husband. But what the hell? They'd head back to the tall and uncut soon, which better suited them both.

When the dimpled schooner had arrived and Nordic had tossed his coin onto the counter, he picked up the heavy glass, sniffed deeply of the malty, hoppy aroma, and took a sip, sloshing it around in his mouth before swallowing.

Damn, that was good!

He wished he could take a barrel of the stuff back to his cabin.

But then he wouldn't get much work done for Deveraux, who would likely find his herds depleted by half by the end of the month. Rustlers with their running irons had really overrun the Never Summers of late. He knew that's why Deveraux hadn't fired him despite his foreman missing a precious toe. The man needed someone to watch over his far-flung herds— the cattle that were so far away from the main headquarters his men couldn't oversee them.

Over the past two months, having run off a good twenty rustlers and shooting three others who'd tried shooting him, Anders had proved his worth.

When he'd taken down half his beer, trying to go slow but not having much luck—damn, he loved the stuff!—his thoughts had turned to the girl. Young woman, rather. Yes, she was all woman. No girl remained in Alexandra Deveraux. A finely setup young woman, she. There'd been an imposing air about her as well as a strange reserve. Anders supposed that's what he and she had in common.

That was likely the only thing.

She'd looked wise beyond her ears. Sharply intelligent. Probably a book reader. Nordic was, too, when he got the time, but doing what he did for a living, there was rarely time. The long winter nights were a good time to read, however. He didn't have much access to books, but over the years he'd managed to get his hands on some volumes by Mr. Shakespeare and he'd read some by Sir Walter Scott and he'd found some interesting nuggets in *The Age of Reason* by Thomas Paine.

His mind had just strayed back to Miss Deveraux —he had a feeling his wasn't the only male mind that did—when a man shouldered up beside him on his left and said, "Is that your dog?"

The man was tall and wore small, round, rose-colored spectacles and the garish suit of a gambler. He wore a high-crowned, flat-brimmed, blue hat.

"That one there?" Nordic said, glancing at Finn glowering up at the gambler. "He's as much mine as I am his."

"Well, he growled at me."

"Yeah, well, he doesn't seem to like you much. Did you step on him?"

"No, I did not. Might have come close to his tail, but I don't think I deserve the look he is presently giving me."

Nordic only chuckled and turned back to his beer and thoughts of Miss Deveraux.

"Call him off," the gambler said.

"What's that?"

"Call him off."

Again, Nordic looked at Finn. The dog sat as before, staring up at the gambler with quiet anger.

Again, Nordic chuckled. "He sure don't like you. Are you sure you didn't step on his tail?"

"I did not!"

"Well, then you got nothin' to worry about. I'll buy ya a beer."

Nordic turned to get the apron's attention but stopped when the gambler said, "If he doesn't stop looking at me like that, I'm gonna *shoot* him!"

"It's apparent to me, *amigo*, that Finn don't like you. And the more I listen to you an' look at you"—*all right, settle down now, Anders*, a voice inside his head warned him, though the rattlesnake in his soul was already too teased to uncoil—"the more I understand why he is. You see, some folks dogs just sense is *bad*. An' Finn senses you're *bad...amigo*!"

He couldn't help himself. He raised his right, clenched fist and slammed it against the fancy Dan's chest. Not hard but hard enough to knock him back a couple of steps.

Finn turned to Nordic and barked once, admon-ishingly.

"Hell, you're the one who started it," Anders told the dog.

The gambler set his black patent half boots beneath him then, his pale face around his large, walrus mustache turning pink. Looking as though his head were about to explode, he fished a pearl-gripped, silver-chased over-and-under derringer out of a pocket of his paisley vest and raised it.

Rage was suddenly a wild stallion galloping inside the man from the Dakota wilds. All previous self-admonishments were buried under his primitive, uncontrollable fury. As the gambler began to ratchet back one of the derringer's two hammers, he bellowed, "Why you...!" and thrust his right foot up in a blur of quick motion.

Motion so quick that no one would have expected a man so large to be capable of such a feat.

The point of Nordic's right boot caught the under-side of the gambler's wrist. There was an audible crack as the bone broke. The gun cracked, smoke and orange flames lapping toward the ceiling into which the .22-caliber bullet plunked. The gambler dropped the derringer and clutched his wrist, which hung at an odd angle in his other hand, and howled like a gutshot coyote.

"Ya broke my wrist! Ya broke my wrist, ya big ape!"

Finn was barking crazily, switching his enervated gaze between his anger-crazed trail mate to the gambler who now held his injured wrist down between his legs, howling. He held the appendage high to show the rest of the saloon and bellowed, "This brigand broke my wrist!"

Nordic was about to turn back to his beer, which he'd only half finished. But before he could go back to the tasty elixir, two big, bearded men ran through the saloon's batwings, both wielding clubs. Each had a deputy town marshal's five-pointed star pinned to his vest.

They both stopped ten feet from the swinging louver doors and the darker of the two, who had a big gut fairly bursting through his hickory shirt, yelled, "Dakota, I told you last time you'd best keep your wolf on a leash when you're in town or you'll spend the night in the lockup an' see Judge Connelly in the mornin' and likely be owin' the city a hefty fine!"

The wolf inside of Nordic had no surcease, however.

Despite Finn's barks behind him, the big Dakotan squared his shoulders at both lawmen and raged, "You just try!"

Finn continued to bark behind him, ordering him to stop.

Rage had closed off all senses in Anders. He knew only rage and the wild energy it fueled.

Nordic ran toward the club-wielding lawmen. He lowered his head and rammed an elbow against each man before they'd realized the size and power of the man they were being assaulted by. Each shrieked and flew to one side. They came up hollering and wielding their clubs. Nordic ducked under the blows. He got low on the big-gutted cuss and bulled him onto a table recently and quickly vacated. He slammed his fist against the man's jaw and then the club wielded by the other deputy smacked across the back of his head.

It was a hard, ringing blow.

Anders tried to straighten but his legs were no longer working.

His knees buckled and he dropped straight to the floor, the room dimming around him.

His last sensation was feeling a cool, rubbery nose sniffing his ear. Finn whined and then Nordic tumbled into a whirling, black vortex of misery he could feel even at the bottom of a well of unconsciousness.

Soon he was vaguely aware of being carried, one man cradling him under his arms, the other one cradling his ankles. Then he was dropped on a cot or bed and there was the ringing, painful clatter of a steel door being shut. A key scraped in a lock. Then silence and howling darkness closed around him once more.

He wasn't sure how long he'd been in the cell when he lifted his head from the moldy pillow and looked around, stretching his lips back from his teeth against the thundering pain in his head. It was either early night or early morning. Pale blue light washed through the window to the right of a fat man who hunkered over the plate in his lap, shoveling food into his mouth and washing it down with deep sips from a speckled tin cup.

He sounded like a cow chewing its cud.

A whine sounded. Anders lowered his head to see

Finn staring out the cell door at the fat deputy eating hungrily.

Nordic sat up, dropping his feet to the floor and rubbing his throbbing head.

"Jesus—you even locked up my *dog*?"

The fat man glanced at Anders and took another sip of his coffee. Setting his cup back down he shrugged a head and shoulder and cut into the steak he was eating with fried potatoes and four eggs cooked sunny side up. "He followed you into the cell and wouldn't come out. So…"

He shrugged again.

"What time is it? Hell, what day is it?"

The deputy hooked a thumb over his shoulder to indicate a clock on the brick wall above a black range.

"Eight thirty," Anders muttered. "What day?"

"Same one you busted Dick Pinto's wrist."

Nordic assumed Pinto was the gambler.

"A month. That's what the book says when you break a man's wrist and assault two deputies." The deputy snorted a dry laugh and glanced once more at his prisoner, the only one in the four cells lined up against the jailhouse's rear wall. Well, two prisoners counting Finn. The man's right eye was swollen shut.

"That looks painful, but I suspect no more painful than my head."

"Serves you right. Shoulda shot you."

Just then boots thumped on the boardwalk fronting the place. The door opened and a tall, gray-mustached man stepped into the jailhouse. He closed the door and crossed to Nordic's cell. A five-pointed town marshal's star glinted on his chest. He crossed his arms on his chest and cocked one hip.

"So…this is the man who broke Dick Pinto's wrist. Anders Nordic."

"He works for Garth Deveraux," the deputy said, still chewing and looking over his shoulder at his boss.

"Oh, I know. We'll see how much longer that lasts." The marshal hooked a wry smile and shook his head. "You're a big son of Satan, aren't you?"

Nordic said nothing.

"Deputy Banner, when did we start locking up dogs?"

"Couldn't get him out of there, Marshal Conagher."

The marshal gave a cruel smile. "Should've shot him and dragged him out to the trash heap out back."

"It crossed my mind," Banner laughed.

Finn showed his teeth and growled at the marshal.

"Never too late," the marshal said through his teeth.

He unsnapped the keeper thong from over the hammer of the Russian .44 holstered on his right hip. Quick as a striking snake, Nordic shot his hand through the bars and grabbed the gun out of the lawman's, pulling it into the cell, aiming at the lawman's belly, and clicking the hammer back.

"I might take that personal," the big man said. "Suppose I give you a pill you can't digest?"

Suddenly, the chief lawman looked as though he'd just encountered an African lion escaped from a circus cage. He raised his hand halfway to his shoulders.

"Hold on, now. Just hold on, big fella. I don't think you want to han—"

He stopped when quick footsteps sounded on the boardwalk fronting the jailhouse. The door opened quickly, and Nordic couldn't have been more surprised to see Alexandra Deveraux standing in the open doorway, her gaze going to Nordic holding the gun on the lawman. Incredulity creased her brow.

"Miss Deveraux," Glen Conagher said, apparently as surprised as Anders was. He turned to face the young woman. "What're you doing here?"

She moved slowly into the office, leaving the door standing open behind her. "What on earth is going on here?"

The deputy glanced at Conagher, who flushed in embarrassment. He looked back at the deputy then turned back to the young woman.

"Just a little misunderstandin'." Anders depressed the Russian's hammer then poked it against the marshal's back, offering it back to him.

Looking deeply sheepish, Conagher took the gun and returned it to his holster.

"What was the nature of the misunderstanding?" Miss Deveraux wanted to know.

"He was gonna shoot Finn," Nordic said.

"Ah."

"I don't allow dogs in the jailhouse," Conagher said.

She glanced at the fat deputy with a caustic laugh. "He's here."

"Hey!" objected Banner.

"Shut it," Conagher said.

It was apparent to Nordic that the young woman wielded a lot of power in this town. Not surprising given the size and prominence of her father's ranch and other business holdings. Nordic had heard he owned several mines and a large interest in a railroad line as well as in several businesses in town.

"Release this man," she ordered. "He's needed on Comanche range. I know my father would agree."

Conagher grew indignant. "Now, look here, Miss Deveraux. He broke a man's wrist earlier and look what he did to Banner's face!"

"I heard in the hotel, where I was having dinner with a prospective business associate, that that man—Dick Pinto," she spat out the name distastefully, "was also going to shoot Mr. Nordic's dog!"

"He growled at him," the deputy said, still obviously hurt by the young woman's insult.

Miss Deveraux glanced around Conagher at Nordic. "Right popular—isn't he?"

Nordic shrugged.

"All right, all right, all right," Conagher said, pulling a large ring of keys off a ceiling support post. "Have it your way, Miss Deveraux."

Finn looked up at Anders and gave a relieved bark.

Reluctantly, Conagher unlocked and opened the door to Anders's cell.

Anders grabbed his hat off the cot, set it gingerly on his tender head, and said, "Come on, Finn."

"Your horse is at the Bronze Boot Livery & Feed," Conagher told Nordic. "Oh, and Dakota, stay out of town. You're no longer welcome." He gave Miss Deveraux a defiant look. "But I got me a feelin' you're not really welcome anywhere."

Nordic ignored the man and he and Finn followed his pretty benefactor out of the jailhouse to where a handsome carriage sat, the fine black in the traces tied to the hitchrack.

"You're in town kinda late—aren't you, Miss Deveraux?" Nordic said.

"I keep a hotel room in town. I'll stay there tonight and head back to the Comanche in the morning."

"Alone?"

"I'm capable of fending for myself, Mr. Nordic," she said, vaguely defensive.

Nordic smiled. "I reckon I saw good evidence of that. Uh, thanks, by the way."

"I didn't do that for you so much as for my father. He needs a good man in the mountains guarding our herds."

"Ah."

She gazed up at him. A flush had risen in her lovely cheeks. He was a little puzzled by that. Did she feel an attraction to him? He thought he'd noticed evidence of that back when he'd first seen her with her father. Now, the well-filled corset of her gown rose and fell slowly, heavily.

He hadn't really thought about what he did next until he'd grabbed her, pulled her to him and, wrapping her tightly in his big arms, kissed her bee-stung lips. She pulled away from him, her hands on his chest. Scowling, she hauled her right hand back behind her shoulder and swung it sharply forward, connecting resoundingly with his bearded face.

A second passed.

Then she was in his arms again, this time of her own accord, kissing him hungrily.

Marshal Conagher appeared in the jail office window left of the door.

He shook his head slowly then retreated back inside the office.

CHAPTER NINE

Nordic and Finn arrived at the line shack long after dark.

Anders's head hurt too badly for him to make supper. Finn had caught a rabbit and devoured it along the trail, so Anders didn't set anything out for the dog, either. He just turned down his lamp and went to bed, waking the next morning after the sun had risen. Odd for him to rise that late but that's what a braining will do for a fella.

He tended Apache and his packhorse, Angus, then saddled Apache and rode toward where the Nordstroms were camped. He'd been on the trail nearly forty-five minutes when the crackle of gunfire rose ahead of him, deep inside the canyon where the Dakota folks were bivouacked.

"Oh, hell—not again!" Anders booted Apache into a ground-chewing gallop, Finn breaking into a hard run beside him.

When he mounted the last rise, he saw a group of

five men once again harassing the Nordstroms. Two of the family were down while the mother struggled with a bearded assailant. The girl was running along the edge of the trees, holding her skirt above her ankles, but the two men chasing her were easily gaining on her. She screamed. The men laughed.

Deveraux's men? Something told Nordic this was another party entirely. These men looked too unkempt for Deveraux riders.

He heeled Apache into another hard run, racing up to the man who had the mother down and was ripping her clothes. Two others stood over him, apparently waiting their turn. Anders shot all three. *Bang! Bang! Bang!*

They were dead.

Such scum didn't deserve a chance.

The two chasing the girl, Sarah, having heard the shots, wheeled toward Anders and drew their sidearms. Nordic checked Apache down quickly and as the two marauders' bullets buzzed through the air around him. He dropped to a knee and dispatched both with the Yellowboy.

They went down hard, yelling.

Both had taken bullets to the chest.

They didn't yell long.

Nordic walked up to them and casually angling the rifle down by his right leg, silenced both.

Sarah was on the ground, on her side, arms crossed on her bulging belly. She sobbed uncontrollably.

"Baby!" her mother cried, running to her daughter, holding the top of her torn dress closed across her torn camisole. She dropped to a knee beside the sobbing girl. "Oh, dear God, baby—are you all right?"

Sarah sat partway up and glanced to where her father and little brother lay unmoving in the shade. She looked at her mother. "I think so. Pa an' Knut aren't moving."

Her mother held the girl, rocking her from side to side, sobbing.

She looked up at Anders standing over them, Finn by his side.

"You saved us," she said. "Again, you saved us."

"Glad I got here when I did. Heard the shootin'."

"You came to…to…"

"See to it that you left."

Mrs. Nordstrom looked at one of the dead men. "Were they Deveraux's men?"

Anders shook his head. "Rustlers. I recognized the leader of the pack—Jack Crawley. I've been lookin' for them. They must have stumbled onto you when they were looking for Deveraux beef."

Mrs. Nordstrom looked at Sarah. "Are you all right, honey?"

Sarah brushed tears from her cheeks and nodded.

"I have to get to work."

Mrs. Nordstrom rose and walked past Nordic and Finn. She stopped and looked down at her dead little boy and then at her dead husband. She was strangely expressionless. She turned away and walked to the covered wagon that sat just a few feet from the bodies. Its tailgate was down. She reached over it and pulled out a shovel. She turned stiffly and walked around to the other side of the wagon.

Nordic frowned at her, puzzled. Finn looked up at him and mewled his own puzzlement. Nordic turned his curious frown on Sarah. "What's she doin'?"

Sarah swabbed tears from her cheeks and sniffed. "She'll be buryin' her dead."

"She can't do that. I'll do that, an' then I'll take you both to town. You couldn't stay here when your pa and brother were alive. You sure as blazes can't stay here now."

"Mr. Nordic…" Sarah said behind him but let her voice trail off as he and Finn walked away, heading for the wagon.

They walked around to the other side of the wagon. Twenty feet beyond it, at the base of the high, conifer-carpeted ridge, Mrs. Nordstrom was just then poking her spade into the ground and using her right, ankle-clad foot to shove it deeper into the sod. Nothing tougher than a pioneer woman. Nordic walked over and wrapped his hand around the spade's splintery, gray handle.

"Mrs. Nordstrom, I'll do that. You're in shock. Besides, this is no work for a woman. The ground is hard. It'll take you forever."

She did not release the spade but only looked at him with a hard, ashen look of determination. Her mouth was tight. Her eyes were lusterless with grief.

"If it takes forever, I'll take forever. I bury my own dead, Mr. Nordic. I buried my family killed by the Sioux in Dakota when I was only thirteen years old.

I've buried two children when Mr. Nordstrom was down with a fever. You may go now, Mr. Nordic. Your work is done here. We're obliged, Sarah and me. I will bury my dead on my new home ground. It's only fittin'."

"Ma'am, you don't understand. You can't stay here. Deveraux wants you out. Besides, this is a hard country. It's no place for two women. For two women and a baby on the way."

"Sarah can't travel. She's been having trouble with the child. We will stay here and build a home here. My brother is on his way here to settle with us. He'll help us cut down trees and build a cabin and to string barbed wire to keep Deveraux off our land."

Nordic was beginning to think the woman was crazier than a tree full of owls. "That's impossible, Mrs. Nordstrom."

"We filed a claim in Camp Collins. This is our homestead. It's all legal-like. We will not be put off our land. Not even by a man like Deveraux."

She shoved the spade into the ground, removed a chunk of sod—a very small one—and cast it away.

Nordic sighed. There was no reasoning with the woman. If she and the girl stayed here, they would die. Maybe he could reason with the girl. He walked around the wagon to find her standing over her dead father. She appeared emotionless now. Dry as a husk. But Nordic knew her heart was heavy with grief. It was too much grief to show.

"Sarah," Anders said as he walked up to her. Finn had run off up the ridge after a squirrel. "You have to talk to your mother. You can't stay here. If you do, you'll die."

Still staring down at her father, who lay belly down in the sage, face turned to one side, his back bloody where a bullet had gone through him from the front, she said woodenly, "If I leave here, I'll die. Me and the baby. The trail up here about killed me. I was sick for days afterwards."

"When are you due?"

"A month."

Anders sighed. He didn't know what to do. He climbed the ridge a few yards above where Mrs. Nordstrom toiled, digging the first of the two graves. He sat down on a rock, rolled a quirley from his makins sack, fired it with a lucifer match from his shirt pocket, and smoked and pondered the situation.

He'd been working line shacks for years. In all those years, the problems had been clear-cut. He'd run off or killed rustlers and even nesters who'd refused to leave. However, most nesters left because they knew it was impossible to stay. Either Nordic would kill them or run them off or the rancher whose land they'd nested on—and which the rancher considered his own if it was not actually his own—did his own killing.

But this situation here with Mrs. Nordstrom and her daughter was damned perplexing.

Four padded feet thumped behind Anders. Finn came up to sit down beside him, looked up at him with a strange understanding of the situation at hand, and moaned. He thumped his tail then stretched his front feet out before him and lay belly down, resting his long snout on his crossed paws.

"What are we gonna do about this, boy?" Nordic ran a hand through the shaggy fur on the dog's back. "I'm fit to be tied."

Finn looked up at him. Again, there was a strange understanding in the dog's eyes. People thought dogs were stupid. But they were not. Nordic had known enough of them, most not even as smart as Finn, but he knew they were deeply intuitive. When he was up, his dog was up. When he was down, his dog was down. Finn seemed to go even farther in this situation.

Nordic looked down the slope. Mrs. Nordstrom was still prying up sod and grunting with the effort. Sarah had come over and sat near her mother, knees raised, her arms around her bulging belly. She stared dully down at where her mother was digging the grave.

Anders drew deeply on the cigarette and blew out the smoke.

Hoof thuds sounded—a handful of riders coming fast.

Oh, no, Nordic thought. *Could this day get any worse?*

Finn rose to a sitting position, raised his ears, and growled.

"Easy, boy," Anders told him. "I'll handle it."

If there was any handling it…

The rataplan of the oncoming riders rose until several men on horseback appeared, riding up to the front of the Conestoga wagon and checking their horses down. They were eight armed ranch hands led by Deveraux's foreman, Wayne Bitterman, who regarded the two women incredulously then gazed up the slope at where Nordic still sat his rock beside Finn.

"Just what in hell is goin' on here, Dakota?"

"What's it look like? The lady is diggin' a grave."

"How the old man an' the boy end up dead?" Bitterman asked. "Me an' the boys heard the shootin' from up north."

"Rustlers led by Jack Crowley."

"Rustlers had to do your work for you—that it?"

Neither the woman nor the girl reacted to the man and his small posse of tough nuts.

"Ride on, Bitterman," Nordic said. "Or you'll be missin' another toe."

Nordic smiled inwardly. The foreman was still sporting a hole in the toe of his right boot. His wool sock shone through it. There was red on it.

"You're gonna be missin' more than that if you don't get these people out of here," Bitterman said, hardening his jaws and narrowing his eyes.

Nordic drew his Colt, gave it a twirl, and cocked the hammer. He rested his right elbow on his right knee, aiming the pistol at the foreman. "Like I said, ride on. I'll handle the situation."

Bitterman jutted his chin out as though begging Nordic to take a punch at it. "You handle it. You got one day. Then I'm gonna handle it and I'll be here with a whole lot more men! Oh, an' by the way—don't think you an' that dog ain't gonna pay for my toe!"

With that, he reined his black-and-white pinto

around and rode through his men. They gave Anders one last, hard look, reined their own horses around, and galloped after their boss, heading back in the direction from which they'd come.

Again, Finn growled, raising his hackles.

Nordic sighed and holstered the Colt.

Mrs. Nordstrom paused in her digging to look up at Anders. She said nothing, just looked at him. Then she went back to work. But she didn't last long. After another half hour, the grave was maybe a couple of feet deep. She stopped digging and leaned forward against the shovel, spent.

"Uh-huh," Nordic said to himself.

He pinched out his second quirley, rose from his rock, said, "Come on, Finn," and walked down the hill. He took the shovel from the woman. She didn't fight him. She just went over and sat down beside Sarah and wrapped an arm around her daughter. They watched as he dug the first grave, which took him an hour to get six feet deep. He dug the second grave beside that one then retrieved the bodies, wrapping them in blankets from the wagon and gentling them into the graves.

Nordic asked Mrs. Nordstrom if she wanted to say anything.

She and Sarah rose and stood between the two graves in which the bodies lay.

"I love you both," the woman said dully. "We'll see you again soon."

Sarah said nothing.

The two women stood watching Nordic filling in

the graves then mounding rocks on them to keep predators out. He fashioned a couple of wooden crosses from branches he found on the forest slope and rawhide from his own saddlebags. He tamped them into the ground at the head of each grave.

The two women watched, tears now dribbling down their cheeks.

Nordic had a big drink of water from his canteen then fetched the women's horses from their picket line. There was a gray and a black, both lean.

"What are you doing?" Mrs. Nordstrom asked him.

Rigging the team with hames and harness he'd pulled out from under the wagon, he said, "Takin' you an' Sarah to my line shack. I can't leave you out here. I can't protect you out here. Even if I tried, I couldn't do my job, and rustlers would likely rob Deveraux blind."

"Deveraux can go to hell!" the woman said.

Nordic looked at her in shock. He'd had no idea she had such a word in her vocabulary. He was impressed by her spleen. But cautiously. If she had her way, she'd likely get her and her daughter and grand-baby-on-the-way killed. He told her as much as he strapped the team to the wagon's doubletree.

"Sarah and I can take care of ourselves, Mr. Nordic."

"Call me Anders."

"Sarah and I can take—"

"No, you can't," he interrupted her, checking the team's cinches and buckles one more time. "If you stay here, you'll die. Bitterman doesn't care that you're two women alone." He gave her a pointed look.

"He'll kill you if to only keep his stubborn reputation intact if nothing else. I can't let that happen."

Mrs. Nordstrom rose and walked over to him. She stared up at him from over his shoulder. "We're none of your business."

"You got that wrong. Since you're on range my boss considers his own, you *are* my business." It was Anders's turn to give the woman a pointed look. "I'm gettin' you both out of here. If you don't come willingly, I'll hog-tie you and throw you in the back of the wagon."

"Sarah can't ride."

"It's not far, an' I'll make it easy on her."

Nordic strode past the woman and crawled into the back of the old prairie schooner. He arranged a soft bed for the girl with feed sacks, quilts, and pillows. He climbed back out and held his hand out to the girl. "Come on, Sarah. You'll find it a whole lot more comfortable in my cabin than out here. An' you won't have to worry about Bitterman's men comin' tomorrow."

Sarah stared up at him. She looked at her mother and said quietly, "He's right, Mother. We can't stay here."

"Your uncle will be along soon."

Sarah shook her head. "Not soon enough." She accepted Anders's hand and let him gently pull her to her feet. He helped her into the back of the wagon and closed the tailgate. "I'll take it slow," he told her.

He tied Apache to the back of the wagon, set his Yellowboy under the wagon's seat, on the driver's side, then walked over to the woman staring at him stubbornly. "You might as well come. Your daughter is." He extended his hand to her. She looked at his hand then into his eyes and saw no give in him.

"I have pots, pans out here."

"I have same in my cabin."

She drew a deep breath, exhaled, and drew her mouth corners down. She accepted his hand, and he helped her up into the driver's box. He climbed into the box then, too, and unwrapped the ribbons from the brake handle. He glanced down at Finn staring up at him dubiously from the driver's side of the Conestoga.

"You want to walk or ride?" Nordic asked the dog.

Finn barked once then leaped up onto the floor of the driver's boot then up onto the leather-padded seat to sit between Nordic and the woman. She did not look at the dog but sat staring straight ahead.

Nordic shook the reins over the team's backs, and they were off.

When they were out in the main canyon and heading straight north toward the line shack another few miles away, trouble showed itself.

CHAPTER TEN

"What is it?" Mrs. Nordstrom asked.

Nordic was staring up the forested ridge on their left.

"Not sure," he said. "Thought I saw a flash on that mountain...'bout halfway up."

"A flash?"

"Like the reflection off a rifle breech...or a spyglass lens." He should have kept that to himself. He was thinking out loud, pondering. Besides, Mrs. Nordstrom was no hothouse flower.

The wagon plodded another few feet when he saw the flash again. It was too bright for the reflection off a rifle breech or a horse's bit or a spur. It had to be the reflection off a spyglass lens. Someone was watching them from the ridge.

He reached under the seat for his Winchester. He jacked a round into the breech, off-cocked the hammer, and set it on the seat behind Finn.

"Oh, dear Lord!" the woman said. "We would have been better off if we'd stayed where we were."

"Doubt it."

Nordic held the team at a slow, steady pace between the base of the high, forested ridge and a broad canyon maybe fifty feet deep on their right. Another steep, forested ridge rose, bathed in the salmon light of the early summer evening, on the other side of the canyon. He kept a close eye on the ridge but saw no more reflections.

He wasn't sure if that was good or bad.

Ten minutes passed. He wished he could speed up the team, but he couldn't do so on account of Sarah. He had to keep it slow, easy. Besides, if horseback riders were stalking him, they'd eventually catch up to the lumbering old Conestoga, anyway.

Tension gripped him.

He took another glance up the ridge and then fear rose along his spine like a cold, steel rod. He saw riders coming down the ridge, riding spaced out about ten feet apart and weaving around the pines, firs, and aspens. There appeared at least five, maybe more.

One of the riders, a mere shadow in the fading light and from this distance of a hundred yards, stopped suddenly. Amid the heavy forest, Anders saw the man leap down from his saddle and drop to a knee. Another sun flash. This time it was definitely the reflection off a rifle breech.

Nordic cursed and steeled himself but kept a tight grip on the ribbons in his gloved hands.

An eerie *whirring* sounded to his left. It kicked up

an atavistic terror inside him but only for a second because then the bullet skidded off his left shoulder, a needling graze, and went caroming off over the team to spang off a large rock ahead and to the right of the trail. Nordic groaned against the bullet's burn, and he leaned forward, losing his grip on the reins as he automatically clamped his right hand over the instantly bloody hole in his shoulder.

The rifle's distant bark reached his ears as well as the ears of those of the two horses. Both reared and whinnied sharply and broke into a hard run, angling off the right side of the trail, away from the rifle's report.

"NOOOO!" Anders bellowed as he reached for reins that were no longer before him but trailing along the ground between their rear, scissoring hooves and the wagon. "Whoa! Whoa! Whoa!" he roared.

To no avail.

The horses heard the barks of more rifles as the horseback riders galloped toward the wagon from the base of the forested ridge.

Mrs. Nordstrom screamed and clung tightly to the seat to keep from being thrown out of the wagon.

Finn barked wildly.

A cold snake of dread flip-flopped in Nordic's belly as the canyon opened before him, growing wider and wider until he could see its entire floor and the thin trickle of a creek streaming a winding course down its center. Behind him, in the wagon's covered box, Sarah groaned and yelled, "*What's happening?*"

Knowing what the wagon's violent bouncing and

fishtailing was likely doing to her and also knowing they were about to plunge into the canyon that was fifty feet...forty feet...twenty feet away had Anders's heart racing even faster than the team ahead of him.

"STOP!" Mrs. Nordstrom screamed, clutching the seat with both hands and leaning forward. "STOP! STOP! STOP!"

She hadn't gotten the last STOP out before the team plunged off the lip of the canyon into dead air. An eyeblink later the wagon's front wheels rolled over the lip, as well...and then the rear wheels and both the team and the wagon were dropping like a stone, Anders feeling himself rising off the seat just before the horses screamed as they smashed into the canyon floor. Nordic flew left off the driver's seat and heard the horrible crunching, crackling roar of the Conestoga smashing into the ground.

Faintly, he heard Finn yelp and saw the dog going airborne, fur rising then slanting in the wind as he flew off the wagon's right side where Mrs. Nordstrom had been but was no longer.

Again, the woman screamed but this was a clipped scream that died suddenly on her lips beneath the horrible but short-lived cacophony of the wagon shattering on the canyon floor.

Anders himself smashed onto the floor of the canyon in sort of a seated position to the left of the wreck, the ground hammering the air out of his lungs and kicking up a furious hammering and burning in his bullet-torn left shoulder.

Groaning, he rolled onto his right side, clutching

his grazed shoulder and trying desperately to suck air into his lungs which felt as small as raisins. As he did, a whimpering sounded. He looked to his right to see Finn moving toward him, limping along, hiking his left rear leg. Sand and dirt clung to the dog's shaggy fur. His head and tail were down. He approached Nordic and touched his nose to Anders's cheek, sniffing as though trying to reassure himself his trail partner was still on this side of the sod.

You made it, boy. Good.

He rolled onto his back, drew a deep breath, finally getting some air into his lungs. He sat up and looked around. The horses lay dead twenty feet away from him. Part of the shattered wagon—so badly broken it hardly appeared a wagon any longer—lay strewn among them, the dirty white canvas lay around them and to one side like a disheveled burial shroud.

A body lay among the ruins.

Nordic cursed and, holding his left arm across his chest, blood oozing from the hole in his shoulder, started to heave himself to his feet. A bullet plumed sand just inches to his right.

Finn yipped and wheeled and ran off several feet before stopping and turning to stare at the top of the canyon wall down which they'd plunged.

Nordic heaved himself to his feet. He saw two men standing at the lip of the canyon wall, staring down at him, both wielding rifles. Their faces were partly shaded by their hat brims. He shucked his .44 and fired three quick rounds toward the crest of the canyon wall just as two of the men who'd ambushed him stepped back out of sight.

Nordic drew the Colt's hammer back again and aimed toward the crest of the canyon wall, waiting for the men to show themselves again. When they didn't, he moved to his left. Keeping one eye on the ridge wall, he stepped through the wreckage of the Conestoga to find Mrs. Nordstrom lying unmoving under the wagon's rear axle, one rear wheel leaning across the axle.

Her eyes stared sightlessly up at him in death. Her arms were thrown out to both sides.

"Ah, Christ!"

Nordic looked around, blinking against the blurriness of his vision. He felt a little unreal, disembodied, and knew the plunge into the canyon had knocked more than the wind out of him. He saw Sarah lying on her side several yards away, to the left of the ruined wagon. Her shoulders moved as she breathed.

She was alive…

Dragging his boot toes, Nordic moved to her, Finn dogging him. Anders knelt beside the girl. She lay with her knees drawn up, her arms around the severe bulge in her belly. She was sobbing, squeezing her eyes shut.

"Sarah…" he croaked out. "Sarah…"

She slid her head slowly from one side to the other. She did not open her eyes.

Somehow, she'd been thrown from the wagon. It had come down at a slant on its right side and that was likely what had thrown her out from under the canvas.

Anders looked around.

An oval-shaped cavern lay in the canyon wall to his right, roughly sixty feet ahead of the dead horses and the wagon and the dead Mrs. Nordstrom.

"Oh, Lord," Nordic said as he snaked his arms under the girl's body and, rising from his knees, lifted her off the ground. "What have I done? What have I done?"

He staggered up along the left side of the horses and the wagon. Keeping an eye on the crest of the canyon wall, expecting the men who'd shot him and hazed the wagon into the canyon to reappear at any moment, he ran in a shambling way to the notch in the canyon wall. There was a slight rise of ground before it. He ducked into the cavern which was broader and deeper than its entrance had made him believe. It smelled gamy but at the moment, he didn't think it was occupied.

The canyon was growing quickly darker behind him, but he had a feeling the men who'd shot him would attempt to gain access to it, to finish what they'd started. He had no idea who they were. He'd had only a quick glimpse of the two men on the canyon wall, and in the fading light their faces had been obscured by their hat brims.

He ducked into the cavern with Sarah in his arms.

He moved to the rear, sloping wall, which was about ten feet from the entrance, and gentled the groaning, sobbing young woman down onto the cavern floor.

"Easy, now, honey. Easy," he said, as he slid his arms out from beneath her.

Groaning, she turned her head toward him and opened her eyes. "What…happened…?"

Anders wasn't sure what to tell her.

He quickly decided on, "We…we had an accident. You'll be okay. I got you. How do you feel?"

She sobbed and shook her head.

That was answer enough for Anders. He was desperately afraid the baby would come. Alive or dead?

The question made his bones quake with horror.

He leaned back on the heels of his boots.

What the hell had he done?

By removing them from their camp, he'd taken them out of the pan and into the fire.

He'd no way of knowing he'd be ambushed, however.

Sitting beside him, Finn looked up at him and gave a little whine of incredulity. Nordic patted the dog's head and ran his hand down the furry body.

"I don't know, boy. I don't know. I'll get us out of this somehow."

His mind went to Apache. He turned his head to peer out of the oval-shaped opening and into the canyon, back toward the darkening hulk of the ruined coach. He didn't remember seeing Apache among the wreckage. The horse must have torn his reins off the wagon before it had plunged into the canyon and galloped away.

That prospect gave him hope.

The Appaloosa was the only way he had of getting Sarah back to the cabin where he could properly tend her. He had to do it himself. In her condition, he couldn't take her to a doctor in Camp Collins. There was no time to fetch one. Besides, he couldn't leave her. He didn't want her to die alone.

Die...

Yes, she'd likely die, Anders thought. Along with her mother...

Rage rippled through him. Just as it did, Finn turned his head to stare out the oval-shaped entrance of the cavern. The dog barked once, loudly, and then he stretched his lips back from his teeth, growling deep in his chest.

"Easy, boy," Anders said, running his hand placatingly down the dog's shaggy back. "Quiet, now."

He twisted around and dropped to his hands and knees. He crawled up to with a few feet of the cave entrance and shucked his .44 from its holster. He wished he'd have thought to retrieve his Yellowboy from among the wagon ruins.

Too late now.

Faintly, the hoof thuds of oncoming riders touched his ears.

The enervated tone of men's voices.

Presently, horseback riders rode into view to Nordic's left. Six men on blowing, tail-switching mounts. They drew back on the mounts' reins, stopping them. They were misty shapes in the growing darkness.

To Nordic's left, Finn gave a low growl.

"No, boy!" Anders placed a hand on the dog's snout and shoved him belly flat to the cavern floor. "Shh!"

Nordic lowered his head. His heart thudded with both rage and apprehension. He wanted to know who his assailants were but at the same time he was badly outnumbered. They could easily shoot him out of the cave. And the girl, too.

They couldn't know he and she were here. It would be too easy for them to finish their savage, cold-blooded work.

"Forward slow, boys," one of them said.

Slowly, they rode forward, moving toward the center of Nordic's field of vision. Anders kept his hand on Finn's head to keep the dog from growling or bark-ing. He could feel the dog's heart beating as fast as his own.

The six riders, shrouded in the deepening twilight of the canyon, began to move off to Anders's right when the girl behind him yelled, "Oh, it hurts!"

All six riders stopped as one.

One turned toward Anders and thrust out an arm and pointing finger. "There!"

Anders thrusted the cocked Colt straight out before him and shot the man out of his saddle.

"Back, back, back!" one of the others cried, wheeling their horses and booting them into gallops back the way they'd come. Their apparent leader yelled, "He's got the advantage. We'll come back for him in the morning when we can see him!"

"Yeah, he's not goin' anywhere," one of the others

said, his voice muffled with distance and the thuds of their galloping horses.

The rataplan of the fleeing men and horses dwindled to silence.

Anders gazed into the canyon through his own pale, wafting powder smoke.

The man he'd shot lay about a hundred feet away. A shadowy, unmoving figure.

His horse had run straight out away from Nordic and had stopped another hundred feet beyond Anders, on the narrow trickle of a stream glinting now in the twilight. The horse turned to stare toward its rider, its reins drooping to the ground.

The leader's last sentence echoed in Nordic's mind.

We'll come back for him in the morning when we can see him!

"It hurts," the girl said again, more softly this time. "It hurts...I th-think the baby's *c-coming!*"

CHAPTER ELEVEN

The girl's words cut through Nordic like the bullet that had torn through his shoulder.

He depressed the Colt's hammer, returned the gun to its holster, and crawled back over to where the girl lay on her back, hands cradling her belly, breathing hard, grinding the heels of her ankle boots into the cavern floor. Rising to a knee, holding his right hand over his grazed upper arm, he looked down at her.

She had her eyes squeezed shut, he could see in the ambient light pushing through the cavern entrance.

"Honey?" he said, breathing heavily with anxiety himself. "Is the baby coming?"

Oh, god—please say it's not! he thought. *I don't have any hot water, no wood for a fire, nor, for that matter, any knowledge of how to deliver a child!*

She opened her eyes, gazed up at him, her gaze bright with misery. "I don't know. He's...kicking around...a lot!" She rolled onto her side, raised her knees again toward her chest. "It hurts!"

"You wait here." *Where in hell do you think she's gonna go??* "I'm gonna fetch us a horse, get you back to my shack."

She groaned, clenching, squeezing her eyes shut once again.

Quickly, Nordic unknotted his bandanna from around his neck, wrapped it around his wounded arm with a groan of his own, and knotted it tightly. He had to get the blood stopped or he'd bleed out. If he died, the girl would die for sure. He turned to Finn sitting nearby, watching him curiously and twitching his ears with worry.

Nordic placed his hand on the dog's head.

"Stay here, boy. Stay with the girl. You understand?"

The dog looked up at him, yipped his acknowledgment.

"Good boy!"

Nordic scrambled out of the cavern, gazing cautiously up at the way the riders had ridden. He could spy no moving shadows in the growing darkness. He moved out onto the gravelly, sandy floor of the canyon. The horse was still where it had been a few minutes ago, idly cropping grass growing up around a boulder on the other side of the rivulet that glistened like a lady's diamond necklace as the stars kindled in the purple arch of the western sky.

The horse was a mere horse-shaped silhouette, starlight glistening on its saddle and bridle bit.

Nordic paused by the man he'd shot and kicked

him over onto his back. He crouched to get a look at his face.

No one he'd seen before.

Anders continued toward the horse, slowing his pace, cooing soothingly.

He held both hands up, palms out, showing the mount he was no threat. "Easy, boy…easy, now."

The horse looked at him and twitched its ears.

Nordic took another slow step…another…

The horse neighed and shook its head.

Nordic stopped. "No, no, no. I'm friendly. I mean you no harm." He wished he had some sugar cubes or part of an apple. He held out one hand as though he did, then continued forward one slow step at a time, his heart pounding anxiously.

Suddenly, the horse whickered and backed away.

Anders stopped.

Then, just as suddenly as the horse had retreated, it lifted its snout toward his outthrust left fist, sniffing. It moved toward Anders, its eyes riveted on his "treat" hand. When it came to within three feet, Nordic opened his hand and grabbed the mount's reins.

The horse retreated, fear showing in its eyes.

"No, no—all is well," he said, and ran his left hand down the horse's snout that had a long, white spot in the shape of Florida running down it.

That seemed to calm its nerves. It stopped pulling on the reins. Nordic was in a hurry—in a panic, actually—but he couldn't help taking a moment to look down at its right shoulder. There was a brand there. Anders slid his head closer to scrutinize it.

It was the Comanche brand—a circle with a wavy line over the letter *C*. A Deveraux horse.

"I'll be damned," Nordic muttered to himself, anger growing in him again.

He'd see about that later, talk to Deveraux later.

Now he had to see to the girl.

He swung up into the horse's saddle and booted it across the rivulet and over to the cavern he had trouble finding at first in the darkness. A spindly cedar grew up to the right of the oval-shaped entrance. He swung down from the leather, tied the reins tightly around the cedar, then climbed the stony mound to the entrance and ducked inside, where Finn sat beside the girl, casting his gaze around Anders at the horse, sniffing.

At first, Nordic didn't think the girl was moving.

When he got closer, her belly rose and fell heavily, and she sucked a sharp breath.

Still alive…

Anders stroked the dog's neck soothingly as he dropped to a knee beside Sarah, snaked his arms underneath her shoulders and knees.

"Going to get you to my shack, honey," he said, lifting her slowly, gently.

She opened her eyes, looked at him in terror, wrapping her arms around his neck. "Where's Mama?" she asked.

"We'll talk about her later. For now, just clear your mind, rest against me…"

"She's dead, isn't she?"

Nordic didn't respond to that. He just told Finn to

stay. He was afraid the horse would kick up a fuss if it saw the dog, which it had likely already scented.

Crouching, the crown of his hat still raking the cavern's low ceiling, Nordic moved to the entrance and outside into the dark night. The horse whinnied again, shook its head.

Anders cooed to it, soothed it.

When it settled down, Anders untied the reins and, cradling the girl in his arms, stepped up gingerly into the leather.

He reined away from the cavern entrance and rode up in the direction the riders had gone, hoping he could locate their trail down to the cavern floor in the darkness.

"Come, Finn!" he said over his shoulder.

The soft thuds of padded feet sounded behind him as did Finn's anxious panting.

"I'm going to die, too," the girl said wanly against Nordic's throbbing shoulder. There was a cold, unsettling fatalism in her voice.

The horse plodded on up the canyon.

"Not if I have anything to say about it, honey," Nordic told the girl quietly.

But he wasn't so sure.

Within the last hour or so, he might have gotten both her and her mother killed.

He should have let Bitterman shoot her and her whole damn family. It would have been faster.

Bitterman...

In the back of his mind, he saw the Deveraux brand on the shoulder of the horse he was riding.

I t took him a while in the starlit darkness, but he found a game trail that led him up out of the canyon.

He was halfway back to the cabin when the thuds of a galloping horse sounded behind him.

Now what…?

He halted the Comanche horse and curveted him to see a riderless horse galloping toward him, reins bouncing along the ground at both sides. Apache stopped a few feet away, lowered his head, and shook it.

Finn barked, happy to see his friend again.

"'Bout time," Nordic said.

Apache snorted and nosed the horse Anders was on, jealous.

"Yeah, well," Nordic said with a snort of his own then booted the Comanche horse ahead.

The girl moaned, pressing her arms taut against her belly.

Nordic rode slowly, not wanting to make Sarah any more uncomfortable than she already was. Nor wanting to bring on the baby, which he had no idea how to deliver. He knew she was in labor, but he was afraid that if she started to deliver out here in the middle of nowhere, she'd die. He had to get her back to the cabin and then—what?

He'd just have to wing it.

She moaned and sobbed all the way back to the cabin. Nordic was a fish out of water. He'd endured many a lead swap and saloon fight, but he'd never endured this kind of stress. He was afraid he'd expire from a heart stroke before he reached the cabin, but then, just as the false dawn was beginning to define the terrain around him, the cabin appeared in silhouette before him. Flanked by Apache and Finn, he reined the Comanche horse to a stop just before it, swung his right leg over his saddle horn, and slid gently to the ground, the writhing Sarah in his arms.

He mounted the boardwalk fronting the shack, fumbled his way inside, and lay the girl onto his cot in the living area section of the small cabin, to the left of the kitchen area and its cupboards, range, and small, square eating table to the right of the door. Immediately, he stoked the stove to life and set a pot of water from the rain barrel outside on it to boil, though he wasn't sure what to do with it.

He'd just been around enough birthings to know that the women helping with the deliveries always seemed to boil water...

"Oh lordy, lordy, lordy..." he said, pacing around the small living area near the cot on which Sarah writhed, moaning.

Finn sat just inside the cabin's open door, yipping with his own anxiousness. Both horses—Apache and the Comanche mount—stood just off the cabin's front boardwalk, necks stretched as they peered inside, noses twitching as they sniffed, both tails switching.

"Oh, no," Anders said when he saw that Sarah's water had broke just after the water on his small range had started to boil.

His knees nearly buckled.

Outside, one of the horses whinnied.

Hoof thuds sounded.

He went to the door, hoping that he wouldn't have to deal with Bitterman now while trying to deliver Sarah's baby. But it wasn't Bitterman who just then reined her fine black gelding to a stop before the cabin.

Yes, her fine gelding.

Alexandra Deveraux…

"Thank God," Nordic said, stepping quickly onto the boardwalk fronting the cabin.

"What is it?" Alexandra said, frowning, drawing firmly back on the black's reins, glancing at the two saddled horses before her.

Finn had come out with Nordic and gave a single, anxious bark.

"Have you ever delivered a baby?" Anders asked the young woman, his anxiousness plain in his voice.

"I helped Mother a few times on neighboring ranches…why?"

Nordic hurried out to her and extended his hands to her. "Come, come…Sarah…Miss Nordstrom…I think she's close!"

Anders reached up and nearly pulled Alexandra out of her saddle.

"Okay, okay," Alexandra said, dropping her horse's reins. "I'm coming, but I—"

"Whatever you can do is more than I can," Nordic said, following the young Deveraux woman into the cabin, tripping over his own feet.

It was only a few minutes later that Alexandra

kicked him out onto the boardwalk. He was pale as a sheet and on the verge of fainting. He collapsed onto the hide-bottom chair to the right of the door, and Finn sat beside him, yipping softly.

All three horses stood close, necks stretched, heads extended toward the big man in the chair, concern in their wide eyes.

Nordic drew deep, slow breaths, trying to calm his racing heart until, only a few minutes after he'd been banned from the cabin, he heard a sharp slap followed by a baby's shrill crying.

Nordic sat back in the chair, resting his head back against the cabin. "Thank God!"

A few minutes later, the door opened, and Alexandra stepped out onto the boardwalk to his right. She held a little, blanket-wrapped bundle in her arms. The bundle gurgled and chortled. Alexandra smiled.

"Would you like to meet your nephew, Uncle Anders?" she said.

He rose, feeling weak in the knees. He peered into an open fold in the blanket and saw the little, pink face inside it, eyes squeezed shut, little pink hands clenched into tiny fists.

"Thank...thank God," Anders said with uncommon relief. "I don't...I don't know...what I would have done if you hadn't..." Suddenly, he frowned at the young woman. "What're you doing... here... I mean, thank God you are, but..."

Alexandra hiked a shoulder. "I usually go for a morning ride. I'm not quite sure, but I ended up... here."

She stared deeply into his eyes.

"Not sure why," she added, "but…"

"I'm glad."

"Are you? I mean…if you hadn't needed help in such a dire situation…?"

"Yes," he said.

"What happened. Where's her family?"

"Long story."

"Wait. I have to get this kid back to his mother."

"How is she?"

"She's fine."

Alexandra pushed back into the cabin. Nordic remained on the boardwalk, feeling as though the shack was strictly female territory now. Alexandra came out a few minutes later, smiling.

"Yes, she's fine. Exhausted, but fine. She's going to need a lot of rest." She looked at his upper left arm, which had stopped bleeding, the bandanna wrapped around it crusted with dried blood. "That arm needs tending."

"It can wait. Just a flesh wound. Sit here," Nordic said, indicating the chair he'd vacated and in which he spent a part of every early morning and late evenings, smoking and drinking coffee, watching the sun either rise or set, alone with his thoughts as he customarily was.

Nordic leaned back against an awning support post and crossed his arms on his chest. "Her pa and little brother are dead. Rustlers led by Jack Crawley."

"Oh, no. Her mother?"

"Dead, too. I was bringing Sarah and her mother

here. We were run off the trail and into a canyon. One of the marauders was riding that horse." Nordic indicated the grullo now cropping the short grass growing between sage shrubs with Apache and Sarah's black twenty feet from the boardwalk. "It has the Comanche brand on it."

Alexandra frowned, incredulous. She rose from the chair, walked out into the yard, and inspected the grullo's right shoulder, running her hand across the brand.

She turned back to Nordic. "I don't understand. Surely none of my father's men would have tried to kill you and the Nordstroms."

"All I know," Anders said, "is that horse has your father's brand on it."

"It must be stolen."

"Could be. But your foreman, Bitterman, has one hell of a sore toe. Or what's left of it."

"You think he attacked you out of revenge?"

"I wouldn't put it past him." Nordic paused as she sat back down in the hide-bottom chair. "Would you?"

Alexandra leaned forward, elbows on her knees clad in black riding trousers, the cuffs of which were stuffed down into the high tops of black boots powdered with fresh dust from the ride here from the Comanche headquarters. "I...don't...know," she said, uncertainly, pressing her hands together.

"How long has he worked for your father?"

"Ten years," Alexandra said. "Give or take."

"Could he have been following your father's orders?"

Alexandra jerked a quick, reproving look at him. "Why would my father try to kill you? He could fire you."

"That was my thought. If it was Bitterman, he was working on his own."

"That doesn't make any sense, either. He wouldn't go against Father's wishes. He has a good job at the Comanche. For a man like Bitterman, jobs like that don't come easy."

"Because he's an outlaw."

"Yes. At least, he was. That's who Father hires. He needs rough men. They're the only ones that keep the Comanche going. This is rough country." Again, Alexandra's gaze locked on Nordic's. "But then, you know that. You yourself, Mr. Nordic…"

"I know. I'm a rough man, too."

"You are."

"So, what are you doing here?"

She looked down at her hands, her extended fingers pressed together. "You asked me that before. I'm still not sure." She looked up at him, scowling. "I'm not sure I want to think too hard on it."

"Might not like what you come up with."

She drew her mouth corners down and nodded.

"Will you stay? For a few hours? I have to bury Sarah's mother."

Alexandra nodded. "Of course. Father will worry, but…"

Nordic nodded then walked over, grabbed Apache's reins, and swung up into the saddle.

"Come on, Finn," he said, as he booted the horse into a trot, heading south from the cabin and into the rough country beyond where a woman from his own home country lay dead beneath a wagon axle.

CHAPTER TWELVE

Nordic retrieved Mrs. Nordstrom's body from beneath the wreckage of the old Conestoga and buried her beside her husband and little boy.

When he returned to the cabin, he was exhausted from lack of sleep and overexertion. Alexandra had stabled her horse with the other whose rider Anders had killed. Anders stabled and fed, watered, and curried Apache then walked around and, after beating the trail dust from his trousers with his hat, entered the cabin.

Finn stayed on the boardwalk, also exhausted. He'd eaten a couple of rabbits while Nordic had dug the grave and erected the cross of branches and rawhide, so he likely wasn't hungry. The dog was good at fending for himself, though Nordic tossed him bones from time to time. He needed to remain self-sufficient, though. Anders was the kind of man who walked the tight rope of life, never knowing when he might fall off.

Alexandra sat at the table with a tin cup of steaming coffee, a meal bubbling in a cast-iron pot on the range. Sarah lay on the cot, asleep, her sleeping baby resting on her chest beneath Nordic's striped trade blanket.

"God, you look exhausted," Alexandra said, rising and hauling a mug down from one of the three shelves over the range. "Sit down."

"Don't mind if I do," Anders said, pegging his hat then slacking into a chair facing the window on the other side of the table. He'd seen enough trouble in his time that he never gave his back to a window nor a door.

Alexandra set a mug of coffee in front of him then popped the cork on a labeled bottle. "Father's good stuff," she said, and added a liberal jigger to his mud.

"Raiding your father's liquor cabinet, eh?" Nordic said.

"Old habit." She set the bottle on the table then walked around and sat across from him, before her own steaming mug. "Nothing like a swallow of good Scotch while sitting around a mountain lake."

"Are you here to stay?"

"Where? Here?" She made a skeptical expression while glancing quickly around the cabin. "Don't get your hopes up!"

Nordic smiled, blew on his coffee and whisky, sipped, and swallowed. "I mean here in the Never Summers. Your home."

They were most definitely her home, Nordic could tell. She was as much a part of these mountains as the pines and firs, the long valleys carpeted in sage and threaded with cobalt streams, the high peaks coated in the ermine of the previous winter's snow.

"Yes. I'm done with cities. Besides, since my mother died, Father is alone. He's not the kind of man who can live alone. He needs someone, though I know from experience he's not easy to live with."

"Yes."

"What about you?"

"What about me?"

"Do you need someone?"

Nordic felt the warmth of a flush rise in his cheeks. He looked down at his steaming mug. "No."

"Are you so certain?"

He looked at her. "Yes."

"A tough man."

"Yes."

She reached across the table, placed her hand over his left one. She glanced at Sarah and the baby asleep on his cot. "Not so tough."

"No, I reckon not," he said with a sigh.

"What are you going to do now?"

He looked at Sarah and the baby. "I have no idea. I'm not used to…to…"

"Getting tangled up in complications like that?"

"Yes."

"It'll come to you. I'd take them but Father wouldn't have it."

"I know."

"Look," she said after a stretched silence, "what happened in town…last night…"

"What about it?"

Alexandra studied him closely, her eyes darting between his, reading him. She looked down at her coffee again. "Don't worry," she said, "it won't happen again."

"It can't," Nordic said, regretting having to say it. He'd never enjoyed a kiss more. He'd felt it had been more than a kiss—it had been something deeper exchanged between them. But he couldn't have her. He just wasn't that way.

She gazed at him for another half minute then finished her coffee and whisky, set the mug down on the table, rose from her chair, and headed for the door. Nordic grabbed her hand and pulled her down onto his lap. He kissed her. She returned the kiss, pressing her breasts against his chest, sandwiching his head in her hands, moaning. Then she pulled away and, the color leaving her cheeks, continued to the door.

She went out.

A few minutes later he saw her out the window, galloping her fine black gelding back in the direction of the Comanche headquarters.

————

Alexandra Deveraux mounted a forested ridge and rode down the other side, seeing the Comanche headquarters in the distance, a mile away. The headquarters, appropriately lit by the sunshine of the western high country, slipped out of sight when she was a third of the way down the ridge. She continued to the valley at the ridge's base and drew rein at the edge of the stream that meandered down the valley's heart, through the fragrant pine and fir forest and which eventually flowed into the Cache la Poudre River several miles to the north.

She swung down from the saddle and dropped the black's reins, letting him drink at the stream. She got belly down on the grassy ground beside the flowing, clear water, and took several deep drafts of the pure, cold stuff herself, hearing the black draw water beside her and swinging his tail contentedly. When Alexandra had slaked her thirst, she rose to her knees and stared into the water, at the reflection of her own face that owned a decidedly perplexed expression.

She couldn't imagine why she'd found herself feeling so deeply, so almost obscenely carnally for the man from Dakota, Anders Nordic. He was everything she'd always avoided—big, rough, gunslinging men. Her father's men. She'd thought that when she'd gone east to finishing school, she'd find a man more to her liking—an educated, cultivated man. A man from a good family.

What she'd found was only frustration.

She'd gone out to the opera with sons of a couple of her father's business associates, but, while they'd been nice and gentlemanly, she'd felt no connection. Both men, her own age and a few years older, polite and well-bred, had left her cold.

Having decided to give up on love, marriage, and children, she'd returned home after her mother's death ostensibly to take care of her father. That had been only part of the reason. She'd decided that she was better off living in the remote reaches where she'd been raised—alone and lonely for the rest of her life.

Part of her saw herself as a monster. She seemed to have no affinity for anyone much less an attraction for the men she'd thought she should have been attracted to. In truth, and to her deep surprise, even shock, she'd found herself tumbling for the big, Dakota-bred loner who lived in her father's remote line shack with his shaggy collie dog he called Finn.

A dog as wild as the man himself.

Earlier in the day, she hadn't realized that she'd ridden out to visit him in his cabin. But halfway there, she'd realized that had been exactly her intent.

It had been a pull as fierce as it was inexplicable to her.

Just as she hadn't realized why she was riding in the direction of the strange man's cabin, she hadn't realized she'd been ready to give herself to him. Yes, give herself to him in the most scandalous of ways— because they were not married.

Young women like Alexandra Deveraux did not give themselves to men until after they were married!

But hers had been a forceful, elemental attraction. And she'd sensed in town the night before that his was for her, too.

But he wouldn't allow himself.

Why?

She knew she was beautiful and desirable. That much had been apparent to her from peering after bathing into the oval, standing looking glass in her bedroom in the Comanche's big, main lodge. As well as by how the men on the ranch had always looked at her since she'd turned fifteen and earlier and had filled out her blouses and formed the right curves in riding skirts and pants.

But Nordic had rejected her.

She found herself feeling not only frustrated but humiliated.

She'd never been to bed with a man. But she'd been ready to go to bed with the big, rough, handsome man from Dakota. In fact, it had been all she'd thought about the night before in the hotel in town, tossing and turning, sleepless, all night long. She hadn't admitted her unseemly desire to herself until she'd been halfway to his cabin, knowing exactly where she'd been heading.

The black lifted its head from the stream and whinnied.

Alexandra's heart quickened.

Hoof thuds sounded as did the sound of crunching pine needles.

She rose and reached for the Winchester carbine residing in her saddle boot.

"Hold on, hold on," said a familiar man's voice above the thuds of a slowly approaching horse.

She turned to peer upstream. A horseback rider rode toward her along the water, weaving among the trees. A tall man rolling with the pitch and sway of the pinto he was on. Alexandra's father's foreman, Wayne Bitterman, still with the hole in his boot and the blood-spotted gray sock showing through it.

Revulsion swept through her. She hated the man like she hated few others. She'd never liked the insinuating way he'd always eyed her. He'd never made any outright moves on her, but she'd known his goatish intentions since he'd come to work at the Comanche nearly ten years ago. She'd never complained about him to her father because she knew how hard it was for Garth Deveraux to keep foremen—mainly due to her father's harsh, uncompromising nature but also because of the danger and hard work on the Comanche range.

Despite her opinion of Wayne Bitterman overall, he did seem to be immune to both her father's hardnosed nature as well as to deadly, slippery rustlers.

Alexandra left the carbine in the boot and turned to see the rangy, flat-eyed, arrogant man riding toward her, swaying with the pinto's lackadaisical walk.

She scowled at him, feeling a flush of annoyance rise in her cheeks. He saw her expression and grinned as he checked the black-and-white pinto down six feet from her. Her black gelding craned his neck to regard the man and the horse behind him.

"Not happy to see me, Princess?" he said, thumbing his dirty cream Stetson up on his forehead, slouching in the saddle, both hands on the horn.

"How dare you take that impertinent tone with me, Bitterman."

He frowned, puzzled, deep lines cutting across his ruddy forehead. "Impertinent. Impertinent. Don't believe I've ever heard that one before."

"Disrespectful."

"Ah." Bitterman chuckled. "Why didn't you say so?" He held her gaze with an insinuating one of his own. "Where you been, your highness?"

She made a sour look. "What business could that possibly be of yours?"

"Oh, it's none of mine. But your father might have an interest."

"What are you talking about?"

"I know where you were. I followed you at least far enough to know where you were headed."

"How dare you follow me! Who do you think you are?"

"Your old man's foreman. You an' I both know how hard my breed is to get way up here...an' how hard we are to keep." Bitterman glowered at her, hardened his eyes as well his jaws behind a three-day growth of blond beard stubble. "Stay away from him. You might think I'm beneath your favor, but he sure as hell is...Princess."

"Stop calling me that. You might be hard to replace, Bitterman, but you're not impossible to replace. If my father knew about our meeting out here" —she crossed her arms on her blouse, masking her cleavage—"and how goatishly you're regarding me—"

"I think he'd be just as interested in the fact of you meeting that wild man from Dakota he has living up in that line shack. He might be a hard breed to get an' keep, but if your father knew your intentions with that uncouth hard case who lives alone with a damn cur, I don't think he'd see him as all that impossible at all."

He straightened his back, his eyes growing harder. "He might have a thing or two to say to you about it, too."

How she hated this man!

Still, she had to admit he had a point. Alexandra's father was very protective of her. Garth Deveraux wanted very much to marry her off to a son of one of his business associates back East. Just because those endeavors had not paid off yet did not mean Deveraux would give up. Garth Deveraux was as stubborn and unwavering as he was hard on his men.

She decided to deflect his attack, narrowing her eyes with suspicion. "Did you run that pilgrim family's wagon into that canyon last night?"

"Don't know what you're talkin' about," Bitterman said, unconvincingly. He gave a sly half smile, though.

"You had a motive, didn't you?" She looked at the bullet-sized hole in his boot.

Bitterman pursed his lips, gave his head a quick wag. "Rustlers, most like. Wantin' to rid these mountains of that big man. Gotta admit, he does a good job." Again, Bitterman shook his head. "But he'll take a bullet for it…eventually. Cryin' shame."

Before Alexandra could respond, he quickly changed the subject.

"You oughta soften up to me, Alexandra. I'm not so bad. Besides, we'd make a good team. Me—I think your old man would abide it."

"Ha! You obviously don't know my father as well as you think you do."

Bitterman reined his horse around and, starting back in the direction from which he'd come, he glanced over his shoulder at her. "We'll see. We'll see." He narrowed a commanding eye at her. "Stay away from Dakota, Princess. If not, things just might go crossways for him…and you."

He turned his head forward and booted the pinto into a trot.

"What's that supposed to mean?" she called behind him, a fresh wave of rage rolling through her.

He said nothing, just kept riding, disappearing into the heavy woods along the stream.

CHAPTER THIRTEEN

Sarah sat up suddenly on Nordic's cot and exclaimed, "Mother!"

Immediately, the baby who'd been sleeping wrapped in a blanket on her chest, started bawling. Nordic looked at the pair from where he stood at the range, scrambling eggs in a cast-iron skillet where bacon sizzled and popped, filling the tiny shack with its succulent aroma.

Nordic had cleaned and bandaged his arm then taken a short nap on the floor after Alexandra had left and had woken famished. Now he removed the skillet from the burner, wiped his hands on a towel, and went over to where Sarah lay with the crying baby. The girl looked at Anders searchingly.

"Where is she?" she asked beneath the baby's screeching wail.

Anders squatted down beside the cot and slid a lock of blonde hair back from the girl's moist, pale cheek. "She didn't make it, honey. I'm sorry. I buried her with your father an' brother."

"Oh, god!" Sarah lay back against her pillow and added her own wailing to that of the baby.

"I'm so lost now," the girl sobbed, resting an arm across her eyes. "I have nothing…no one! I wish we never would have left Dakota!"

"You have your son, Sarah. You have to stay strong for him."

"I can't! I'm weak! My heart is broken."

Nordic picked up the crying, blanket-wrapped child and held him against his chest. It was an awkward maneuver. He'd never held a child so young before, and he wasn't sure how to do it. The baby seemed so fragile, as though his little bones would break if the man from Dakota squeezed him even just a little too tight.

"I'll take the boy. You're exhausted. When you're ready, I'll fix you a plate of food."

"Oh, god…how can I eat?" Sarah wailed. "My family is dead!"

"Not all of them." Nordic knew it was pointless to try and reason with her. Of course, her heart was broken. Her grief filled the cabin. He had to let her cry, express her sorrow. In the meantime, he'd hold the baby and have a cup of coffee. He'd eat later. His own hunger was abated by Sarah's sorrow.

She'd feed the baby for now with the milk from her bosom. Nordic didn't know when a newborn needed something more. Sarah's mother had probably schooled her daughter in all of that which was so foreign to Nordic, who felt especially big and lumbering as he walked to the table with the tiny child in his brawny arms.

He held the child in a chair at the table, rocking him gently and cooing to him until he finally fell asleep.

After a half hour or so, Sarah finally exhausted herself, as well, and slept. Anders laid the baby on her chest, giving him access to her breast, then sat down at the table and ate. After he'd eaten and cleaned his dishes with water from the rain barrel on the porch, he went outside and sat with Finn. He smoked and drank another cup of coffee to which he added a liberal jigger of whisky to help dull his jangled nerves and to assuage the burning pain in his arm, though the painful arm seemed the least of his troubles after all that had happened.

The wagon's plunge into the canyon by men he hadn't gotten a good look at. The death of Mrs. Nordstrom and Sarah's delivery of the baby, which Alexandra had expertly assisted her with.

Alexandra…

She was a problem, too.

For some reason, the young woman wanted him. She was likely fascinated by him because he was so different from her—and her, him. And, he had to admit, he wanted her. She was beautiful and cultivated and everything else he wanted. To him, she was as exotic as he was to her.

How could he possibly deny her?

But he had to for both their sakes. Such a union

would never pan out. Besides, her father would be furious at them both. Nordic knew that he was nothing more than a cowhand and a hired gun to Garth Deveraux. Deveraux's daughter was a precious jewel only the best, most educated, cultivated man could have. The thought of Nordic and Alexandra Deveraux was laughable now that he thought about it.

Finn sat beside Anders, resting his chin on the big man's knee, staring up into his face. The dog sensed the turmoil in his trail partner's mind.

The afternoon and evening passed slowly.

Sarah and the baby slept.

When Sarah woke around eleven that night, Nordic fed her some broth, convincing her she needed to keep her strength up for the baby. She ate a few spoonfuls then fell back asleep. Anders fed Finn some bacon then brought the dog inside, where he slept curled next to Anders on the floor, as though to sooth him.

The dog did just that. Since they'd thrown in together a few months ago, the man always slept better when the dog was near. He knew Finn slept better when the man was near.

Anders slept good and hard and woke at dawn refreshed.

The baby cried, wanting to be fed. Sarah woke and fed him, sitting up on the cot, wrapped in a blanket, resting back against the cabin's log wall. Anders scrambled more eggs and fried more bacon and got Sarah to eat a few bites of each and drink a little more broth. Sarah changed the baby at the table while

Anders, having eaten a big plate of food himself, cleaned his dishes.

When Sarah and the boy had returned to the cot, he asked if she felt well enough to stay alone. She nodded. "We'll just sleep," she said, her face drawn from anguish and the misery of the hard labor. Anders thought it a miracle that she and the boy had survived and that both were doing well—at least, physically. It would take Sarah a long time to get over the misery she'd been through.

Nordic kissed the girl's forehead, grabbed his hat, pistol, shell belt, and rifle, and, calling to Finn, left the cabin and headed for the stable flanking it. A few minutes later he left the yard astride Apache and trailing the saddled Comanche horse by its bridle reins. He was halfway to the Comanche headquarters when he had the ominous sense—a prickling under his shirt collar—that he was being watched.

Maybe followed.

Finn and Apache seemed to sense it, too, lifting their heads and sniffing the breeze.

Anders stopped the horses and hipped around in his saddle to peer behind him.

Nothing but the forested ridges rising between him and his cabin on a higher ridge than the other ridges around it. Just the same, he loosened his rifle in its sheath, pulled his Colt from its holster to check the loads, placing a live one into the chamber he usually kept empty beneath the hammer, and rode on.

An hour later he rode up the hill through pines and into the headquarters of the Deveraux Comanche

Ranch. The yard was empty save for a blacksmith and the bunkhouse cook boiling breakfast dishes in a big caldron suspended from an iron tripod.

No, not quite empty.

Alexandra Deveraux stood on the broad veranda, regarding him questioningly.

Nordic put Apache up to the base of the porch steps and said, "Is your father home, uh, Miss Deveraux?"

Just then the two big oak doors opened behind her and the impressive figure of Garth Deveraux stepped onto the porch frowning incredulously. "Go on inside, Alexandra," he said without looking at her.

She turned and walked into the lodge.

"What are you doing here, Mr. Nordic?" the rancher asked, gruffly.

Nordic tossed his head to indicate the grullo standing behind him. "Do you recognize this horse, Mr. Deveraux?"

Deveraux frowned. "Should I?"

"It has your brand on it. This was a horse of one of the riders who drove the Nordstrom wagon into a canyon, killing Mrs. Nordstrom."

"I buy, sell, and trade horses all the time, Nordic. I can't be expected to remember them all!"

"No, I s'pose not. You might as well keep him since he has your brand on him...and his rider is dead."

He dropped the horse's reins, pinched his hat brim to the man, and swung Apache back into the yard, heading for the main trail leading out of it.

"Come, Finn!"

He was a mile or so back in the direction of the cabin when, trotting ahead of Nordic and Apache, Finn suddenly turned to a pine-stippled ridge on his right and barked angrily.

"Come on, boy!" Nordic said, immediately swinging Apache toward a rocky hillock on his left.

More damn trouble…

They'd just started running when a bullet blew only a few feet to Finn's right. The dog yipped and jumped and kept running, tail down. They ran around the backside of the hill as several more bullets plowed into the top of it followed by the barks of the rifle that had fired them.

Nordic shucked his rifle and leaped out of the saddle.

Finn hunkered down beside him as he raised his rifle over the lip of the knoll, racked a round into the breech, and fired in the general area where pale powder smoke wafted. Jacking and firing the Yellow-boy, he sent four rounds caroming toward the general area of the bushwhacker hunkered down in the pines.

Silence.

The thuds of a galloping horse sounded. The top of the ridge was bare of trees. The bushwhacker thundered out of the forest and dashed up the twenty feet toward the top of the ridge. Just before he reached the ridge crest, he turned his head to glance back behind him.

Then he crested the ridge and dropped the opposite side.

Bitterman.

Anders hadn't gotten a good look at the Comanche foreman, but he knew the bushwhacker was him. Anders knew that pinto.

Finn barked. The dog knew it was Bitterman, too.

The man from Dakota mounted his Appaloosa and continued back toward his cabin now being shared with a grieving young woman and her baby.

CHAPTER FOURTEEN

Wayne Bitterman's nerves were shot.

After his bullet had narrowly missed Anders Nordic—that damn mutt had alerted him of Bitterman's intentions, and the man on a fast horse had narrowly avoided it. Bitterman worried about the big man from Dakota. He'd never worried about any man before. But he worried about Nordic. The man was capable of foiling his best laid plans. What's more, Bitterman was well aware of Deveraux's punishment for rustlers. Having performed those punishments personally, he knew how ugly they were.

Beatings, shootings followed by a long, slow hanging, the bodies left to dangle as a warning to other would-be rustlers.

After his bullet had missed Nordic, Bitterman remained on the range till after dark. Now he descended the southern ridge and entered the Comanche headquarters from the back. He rode well around the main house then stabled his horse and continued to his foreman's cabin flanking the bunkhouse where he lived off by himself, away from his boss's prying eyes.

He leaped up on his small front stoop and stopped dead in his tracks when a woman's voice said, "Where've you been, Wayne?"

Her voice so startled him that he fell back against the front of the log cabin, his heart racing, sweat oozing from his pores.

"Christ," he said in a strangled voice, "what in hell are you doing here?"

"You asked me where I'd been. Now I'm asking you."

"I was out…out on the range. I think rustlers might be preying on the small herd in Comanche Canyon."

"All by yourself?"

"The men work hard. They need their sleep."

"How charitable of you."

His voice hardened and became threatening. He needed to get the upper hand. "I won't be deviled by you, Miss Deveraux."

"Why not? You deviled me earlier." Her voice was frustratingly cool, insinuating.

"Look," he said, "I don't know what you're doing here. You made your thoughts about me plain as day. If your father caught you here, he'd shoot us both."

"He won't. I'm as stealthy as you are."

Bitterman frowned, puzzled. "Stealth…"

"Never mind. Buy a girl a drink?"

Now he glowered at her in exasperation. "You've

never wanted to come into my cabin before. Why tonight?"

"We have a matter to discuss." She glanced at the bunkhouse. "I don't want any of them to overhear in case they have a need to step outside to make water."

"What's this 'matter'?"

"Buy a girl a drink," she said, commandingly.

He looked around quickly, making sure they weren't being watched. "All right, all right." He flipped the latch on the cabin door and stepped inside.

She followed and closed the door on the cool night behind her. She took a seat at his small, crude table. He pegged his hat and denim jacket then pulled a bottle down from a shelf on the back wall of his small, crude eating area. When he turned to the table, he saw that she was dressed in a buffalo robe and buffalo hide slippers. He didn't think she wore anything under the robe. Her hair tumbled down her shoulders, glistening in the moonlight angling through the window in the wall to her right. He poured them out each a shot of whisky from an unlabeled bottle then sat and ran his hand through his hair.

"All right—what's this about? I know you don't want to have anything to do with me and my mattress sack and that you came out here dressed like you are and with your hair down to bedevil me."

She sipped her whisky, swallowed, and set the glass down. "Where do you go at night? When you ride out alone from the headquarters?"

Bitterman felt the blood rise in his cheeks. He tried to hide it by throwing back his own whisky then refilling his glass from the unlabeled bottle. His mind raced, searching for an explanation. It landed on one. He didn't know how convincing it would be, but...

"Suppose I have a woman. Would that be so hard to believe?"

Alexandra smiled. "A rancher's daughter?"

He took another deep sip of his whisky. "Something like that."

"Why so surrep...why so secretive?"

"Maybe her old man doesn't want her with a common saddle bum. You could understand that, couldn't you?"

"I think you're lying."

Exasperation rose in Bitterman. "What—do you stay up all night staring out your bedroom window?"

"Pretty much. I've never been able to sleep much."

"Me, neither. That's why I go riding."

"After riding all day?"

Bitterman shrugged.

"Were you one of the riders who ran the Nordstrom wagon into that ravine. Did you try to kill Nordic?"

He slapped the table in anger. "Hell, no!"

She planted her elbows on the table and leaned forward, gazing at him saucily. "Was it because he...or his dog...shot your toe off?"

"I wasn't part of that group, dammit, Alexandra. Don't go gettin' your suspicions up about me. I've been a good man for your pa for a good many years. Long before you went east to get all educated."

"Well, I did get all educated, and now I have a

suspicious mind." She polished off her whisky and poured another jigger into it. She polished that off and rose from her chair.

"Where in blazes did you learn to drink like that?"

She quirked a wry smile. "I am my father's girl, after all." She walked to the door and turned back to him. "Just know that while you have your eye on me, Wayne"—she narrowed one eye—"I have mine on you."

"Oh, go to hell!"

She laughed, opened the door, and left.

Bitterman polished off his whisky and ran his hand through his hair again in frustration. That girl was way too observant for her own good.

She might have to take a "rustler's" bullet someday when she was out gallivanting around the mountains, her nose in the air.

"Oh, hell!" he exclaimed.

He kept seeing that hang noose, felt it growing gradually tighter around his neck.

———

W hen Alexandra returned to the main lodge, she could hear her father's snores from the second story. As he was an early riser, he turned in early.

Alexandra went upstairs and once in her bedroom she pulled a chair up to the window that faced the bunkhouse. All its windows were dark. She spied no movement around the bunkhouse itself, but she saw a shadow move in front of the main stable. The shadow took the shape of a horse and rider, the rider wearing a long duster. The horse's bit glistened in the moonlight.

The rider, who likely lived in the cabin behind the bunkhouse, swung east around the barn, put the horse into a trot and left the yard, quickly swallowed by the night.

Alexandra nodded slowly, pensively.

Bitterman.

Where did he go at night?

One of these nights she was going to find out.

———

A nders found Sarah looking much lighter and happier in the cabin with her baby.

To give them room to get to know each other, after supper, he headed out with Finn to take a swim in a nearby creek, despite the night's thickening darkness. Swimming in clean, cold mountain streams was his way of relaxing at the end of a long, hard, perplexing day. It was both relaxing and invigorating. He always slept better afterwards.

Finn sat on the bank watching him, bushy tail curled around him.

As he kicked around in the frigid, spring-fed stream, Finn growled.

Anders turned to the dog.

He was gazing up at the crest of a low ridge a hundred yards away, growling and snarling softly.

Nordic followed the dog's gaze.

"What is it, boy?"

Then he saw him—a horseback rider sitting the
crest of the ridge and silhouetted against the moonlit
sky. As Nordic stared at the man, curiosity and apprehension rippling up his back, the man reined the horse
around and they disappeared down the ridge's far side.

Anders grunted.

Bitterman, no doubt.

He was out mighty late.

Nordic stepped out of the stream, toweled off,
dressed, and headed back toward the cabin. Finn was
close on his heels.

Anders stepped into the cabin to find Sarah and the
baby were asleep. A single lamp burned on the table.

Nordic barred the door and leaned his rifle against
the wall beside it.

He was up early the next morning.

Sarah was up, too, rocking the baby in a chair by
their cot. The child gooed and gawed, content. Nordic
fried them a breakfast of eggs and bacon, though he
had nothing for the baby. He'd ride to town and fetch
some milk and a few other supplies. He told Sarah to
bar the door and keep low. Then he and Finn went out.
Nordic saddled Apache and in the pearl dawn light
rode up to the top of the ridge where he'd spied the
previous night's rider.

He took a long look around at the rolling, forested
terrain stretching to distant mountains. It was a vast
land. Nordic sensed the secrets it kept. He had a strong
feeling Bitterman was part of the mystery.

When Anders was relatively certain no one else

was around, he put Apache back down the ridge, and he and Finn headed for town.

They were on the trail over an hour when Nordic spied movement off to his right a quarter to a half mile away. He stopped Apache and reached back into his saddlebags for his spyglass, held it to his eye, and adjusted the focus. Horseback riders were herding cattle into a canyon, tracing a circuitous route down the steep slope. Anders saw only two men but there were likely more. The cattle were kicking up a large dust cloud.

Soon they were gone.

Nordic was off Deveraux Range now, but still he was curious. Could be cowboys and cattle from a nearby ranch. He'd check it out on his way back from town.

CHAPTER FIFTEEN

Nordic followed the canyon of the Cache la Poudre River—no prettier or faster moving river, dropping down the canyon's steep incline, had he ever seen. He followed the trail into the town of Camp Collins, visited the mercantile, and headed straight back. He needed no more town trouble. Finn couldn't have agreed more. The dog didn't even enter the bustling, little burg but waited for Anders on the outskirts.

Just as Anders did, the dog had had his fill of town trouble.

After another hour's ride, Anders found himself at the spot in the trail where he'd spied the men herding the cattle into the canyon. He reined Apache off the trail and over to the canyon mouth. The trail was steep and marked with the tracks of cattle and horses. Nordic had explored the canyon before—the same one that passed by his cabin—and knew a stream bisected the canyon, so the cowboys might have only been leading the cattle to water.

Still, he was curious and decided to follow the tracks, Finn trotting along beside him, tongue drooping over his lower jaw.

Anders rode through the bottom of the canyon for forty minutes when he heard the lowing of cattle on the mountain's chill breeze. He turned Apache into some rocks and dismounted, ground tying the horse.

"You stay, boy," he told Apache. "Come on, Finn," he said to the dog. "Let's check it out."

He shucked his Yellowboy from its scabbard, and man and dog tramped off south along the canyon floor, staying close to the cover of pines, firs, and large rocks to his left. When he heard men's voices beneath the cattles' lowing, he climbed into a niche in the rocks, crouched behind one large rock, and edged a look over the top. The cattle were in and along the stream fifty yards away. Four men sat their horses at the edge of the stream, the mounts drawing water. One of the saddled horses didn't have a rider.

Nordic had just made this observation when a gruff voice rose on his left.

"Hold it right there, Dakota man!"

Anders turned to see a tall, slender, bearded cowboy standing on a ledge above him, holding a Winchester carbine on him.

The man glanced at the men along the stream and yelled, "Hey, fellas, we got us a visitor!"

Finn barked at the man, growling.

"Easy, boy," Nordic said. "Stay with me."

"That's right," said the man with the carbine. "Stay there or you'll buy yourself a bullet, you mangy cur."

Finn barked once more and fell silent.

Meanwhile, Nordic heard the clomp of hooves and peered over the rock before him. The other four riders were moving toward him, two loosening pistols in their holsters. There was one bearded, stocky man in his forties. The other three were younger, their eyes hard beneath the brims of their Stetsons.

They reined up on the canyon floor and glared up at Anders.

The older man said, "What're you doin' skulkin' around in the rocks, Dakota man?"

Anders had seen these men on the range before and in a saloon in town.

"Just curious is all," Anders said.

"This ain't Deveraux graze," said one of the younger men. "This is Half-Moon graze. You're trespassin'."

"Just thought I'd see if you were bein' rustled," Nordic said. "Take it easy—my dog and I will be on or way."

He and Finn started down out of the niche. When they were on the canyon floor, the four men before him continued to glare at him. The one who'd been above him with the carbine followed him down out of the rocks and stood behind him, carbine aimed at his back.

Nordic glanced at him. "No need for that, friend."

"I'll be the judge of that!"

The older man said, "You know, there ain't many

folks around here who like you. They think you're uppity."

"Just doin' my job."

One of the younger men, with hard blue eyes and a long, hooked nose, said, "They say you can fight."

Nordic didn't respond to that. He wasn't here for trouble. He had a short fuse, and he didn't want to have it lit.

The older man glanced at the three younger men on his right. He quirked a wry smile. All four dismounted. The man with the carbine stepped up to Anders and jerked the Yellowboy out of his right hand and tossed it away. He pulled the pistol out of Anders's holster and tossed that away, as well.

That lit Anders's short fuse.

The dynamite keg it was attached to exploded.

And whipped around, jerked the carbine out of his hand, and slammed his big right fist against the man's face. He heard the jaw break. The man screamed and stumbled backward to drop to the ground on his butt.

Nordic rammed the butt of the man's own rifle into his gut, evoking a deep, miserable grunt.

Finn barked angrily at the broken-jawed cowboy.

"Get him!" roared the older man.

As Anders started to turn toward them, one of the younger men slammed a pistol barrel against his left temple. The sharp pain made Anders even angrier. It made Finn angry, too. The dog was barking and snarling constantly now. Anders stepped forward, grinding his teeth against the burning pain in his head, and slammed his fist against the younger man's face, splitting his lips so that they looked like a smashed tomato. The young man screamed and stumbled back, dropping his pistol.

The older man said, "Why, you big son of a bi—" and buried a fist in Anders's belly before kicking him in the groin. Anders heard the air rush out of his lungs in a loud *whoosh* as he jackknifed forward over his aching privates and dropped to his knees. Another younger man smashed his fist against Anders's right eye and then two others hurried around behind him and, pinning arms behind back, pulled him to his feet. They held him tight while the older man went to work with his fists on Nordic's nose, cheeks, lips, and belly.

The older man had a powerful punch, and each blow sent agony caroming through Anders.

There was the bark of a revolver, and Anders heard Finn yelp.

Had these thugs shot his dog?

If so, they'd better kill him, too...

The older man continued to work on Nordic until his vision dimmed and consciousness leached out of him. He dropped to the dirt first on his knees and then on his belly and lay still, the blackness of night filling him.

————

An hour later, consciousness returning, he felt a cold nose pressed against his cheek, heard a low mewling. Nordic rolled onto his back. He was surprised to see Finn standing beside him, looking down at him, ears pricked, tilting his head from side to side.

"Well, I'll be hanged," Nordic grunted. "You're still kickin', ol' buddy."

He saw a little patch of blood on his rump, but it appeared to be a graze.

The dog was in better shape than Nordic was. His face and groin were on fire, and his belly ached badly. He licked his lips, tasted the blood.

"Damn."

He tried several times to heave himself to his feet, but he was so sore and weak it took him several more times before he was finally standing, feeling disoriented and off-balance. With a grunt to pick up his hat. With two more grunts he retrieved his rifle and pistol.

"Come on, Finn," he said with another grunt and started toward where he'd left Apache, hoping the Half-Moon vermin hadn't stolen him.

If so, they knew the penalty for horse stealing.

Apache was where Anders had left him. Anders patted the loyal mount, slid his rifle into its boot, and mounted gingerly, hearing his joints pop.

"Come on, Finn," he said mostly out of habit. The former stray would follow Nordic to the end of the earth. "Let's get back to the cabin and take a load off."

Finn barked softly and wagged his tail.

They rode up out of the canyon and resumed their trek for their temporary home. Nordic paused at the stream to bathe his bloody face in the chill water, groaning against the burn in the various and sundry cuts and bruises. One eye was nearly swollen shut.

Finished, he mounted Apache and rode around the cabin to the stable, unsaddling the horse and leading him into a stall. He fed and watered him. Then Nordic pulled his possibles sack and he and Finn walked back to the front of the cabin.

Nordic knocked softly on the door in case the baby was asleep.

He heard the scrape of the locking bar being removed from its brackets.

Sarah opened the door, looked him up and down, gasped, and closed a hand over her mouth. "My god!"

"I've been worse."

Sarah stepped back and Nordic and Finn went inside the cabin. The baby was on the cot, fussing softly.

"Sit!" Sarah ordered, pointing at a chair at the table then grabbing a pan off a shelf. "I'll heat water."

"I washed at the stream."

"You need warm water and whisky."

"Well, I won't argue with whisky," Anders said, slumping into a chair facing the window.

Sarah returned with a pan of rainwater from the barrel on the porch, set the pan on the range, and chunked wood into the firebox. When she had the stove stoked, she removed Anders's firewater from a shelf over the dry sink and set it on the table before him.

"Drink!"

Anders glanced at her with a half grin on his bloody mouth. His nose was bleeding, too, as was most of the rest of his swelling face. "Will you marry me?" he asked the girl ironically.

"Don't drink too much. I'll need some for the water."

He groaned at the imminent burn. "Now, that's a waste of good Who-Hit-John."

"Do you have a needle and catgut."

Nordic sighed. He was going to get the full treatment whether he wanted it or not. He hooked his thumb over his shoulder. "In that tomato crate under the sink."

She retrieved the leather sewing kit and came to the table. "Rustlers?" she asked, starting to thread the needle.

"No, but just as bad. It seems I'm not well-liked in these environs. But then I'm generally not liked in any environs."

She closed one eye to thread the needle. "I like you just fine. Robert does, too."

Nordic glanced at the baby swathed in heavy blankets. "Robert?"

"I thought of it last night. My grandfather's name."

Nordic took a deep pull of the hooch. "Good one."

When the water was steaming, she poured a goodly portion into a porcelain bowl, dropped two rags into the bowl, set the bowl on the table, and poured a good third of the whisky into the water.

"Hey, hey!" Anders objected. "You're gonna burn my face off my head!"

Sarah ignored him, sunk one of the cloths deep into the whisky and water, and wrung it out. She looked at his face and winced. "Where to start, where to start?"

During the next hour, he nearly passed out twice from the burn of the whisky and the sutures. But she was doing a thorough job as delicately as possible.

"Where'd you learn your doctorin'?" Nordic asked her, groaning as she poked the needle and thread through his bloody left brow.

"From Mamma. When you grow up on a farm with no doctors around, you just have to, that's all. Papa sunk an axe into his leg and would have died if not for Momma's quick action." Tears glazed her eyes as she remembered her family.

Anders ran a tender thumb across her cheek.

She brushed a hand across her other cheek, wiping away a tear and continued the doctoring.

Under the table, Finn gave a sad yip for his agonized trail partner.

When Sarah finished with Anders's face, she said, "Are you injured anywhere else?"

"No place you're gettin' to."

She gave a dry chuckle.

CHAPTER SIXTEEN

A ided by frequent sips of the whisky, Anders slept fitfully on the floor beside Finn.

Twice he woke to Sarah's sobs issuing from the cot where she held little Robert on her chest. She was thinking of her family, Nordic knew, who had never lived to see her baby. She was probably crying about the uncertainty of hers and her baby's future.

He let her cry. She had to get it out.

He took another pull from the bottle and fell back asleep.

A horse's whinny woke him midmorning. Instantly, his .44 was in hand, cocked and aimed at the door. Sarah was frying eggs, bacon and, judging by the smell, she had cornbread in the oven. The cabin was aromatic with the fragrance of fresh coffee.

Sarah leaned over the table to look out the window then turned to the groggy Anders. "It's Miss Deveraux. She fancies you, I think."

"No accountin' for taste." Anders threw off his blankets.

Finn ran to the door and barked.

Anders rose heavily. His injuries were still on fire despite the hooch.

He stepped into his boots, walked to the door, and walked out onto the porch.

Alexandra's reaction to his face was much as Sarah's had been. She gasped, widened her eyes, and covered her mouth with a leather riding glove.

"Good Lord—what happened to you. Was it Bitterman?"

Anders shook his head. "Half-Moon."

"Why?"

"I reckon they don't find me all that likable."

Alexandra shook her head in anger. "Frank Ehrlich is a ne'er-do-well. My father has been at odds with him for years. Do you want me to have Father send riders?"

"Nah, I'll fight my own battles. You can see how good I am at it." Nordic beckoned to the young woman. "Light an' sit a spell. You're just in time for a late breakfast."

"Father and I had pancakes and eggs."

"Well, coffee, then."

"Don't mind if I do."

She swung her right leg over her saddle horn and dropped straight down to the ground. She wore a black Stetson with a chin thong, wool sweater over a white blouse, and a black skirt and boots. Her chestnut hair glistened in the midmorning sunshine.

Sarah greeted the young woman as she and Nordic entered the cabin.

"You're just in time for breakfast if you haven't already eaten."

"Thank you—I have." Alexandra went over to greet little Robert who grinned up at her. "He is a darlin'!"

"His name's Robert, after Grandfather," Sarah said, filling three tin cups at the table. "Surely you'll have coffee."

"Of course."

When Alexandra and Anders had taken seats, he blew on his coffee, sipped, and asked the young woman what had brought her.

She drew a deep breath and let it out slowly. "I came to warn you about Bitterman. I think he's up to no good. He rides out well after dark every night. I've discussed it with Father but he's on Bitterman's side. He believes every rancher in rustling country needs a merciless foreman."

"He might have a point. He was here last night, perched on that ridge yonder. I do believe he has it in for me, though it's all Finn's fault." He looked down at the dog, who wagged his tail.

"Of course he does, but I don't think it's as simple as that."

"Sarah?" Anders said, incredulous.

Sarah had just placed a steaming plate of ham and eggs in front of Nordic. She looked at Alexandra apprehensively.

"No, it's not her. He knows he has nothing to fear

from her. It's something else, Anders. It might have something to do with you and me."

Nordic stopped shoving food into his mouth to look at Alexandra curiously.

"He follows me. The other night, he was waiting for me."

"Ah. He's set his hat for you, that snake."

"Yes."

"Want me to kill him?"

"Of course."

Sarah laughed.

Nordic said, "I'll ride with you back to the Comanche. Maybe he'll show himself and I can blow another toe off."

Alexandra smiled.

Sarah sat timidly down at the end of the table to Nordic's right and shuttling her incredulous gaze to him and the Deveraux woman, began eating and sipping her coffee. Robert had gone back to sleep. He made no sounds. A content baby despite the situation...

When he and Sarah had finished eating and Alexandra had finished her coffee, Nordic grabbed his fringed buckskin jacket and rifle and donned his hat. He gave Sarah, who was cleaning up, a kiss on the cheek. "I won't be gone long."

"You really should stay here and sleep. You have to be weak. You lost a lot of blood, and you're pale."

"Later."

She nodded and continued piling dishes in the sink.

He turned to the door beside which Alexandra stood.

"Are you sure you should leave them?" she asked.

"I don't think Bitterman even knows they're here. Besides, not even he is depraved enough to bother a young mother and her baby."

He opened the door and stepped aside to let Alexandra pass. He turned to Sarah, winked, said, "Come on, Finn," and left, the dog following him onto the porch.

Anders and Alexandra had ridden a hundred yards from the cabin when, riding to his left, she turned to him abruptly, a grave seriousness in her gaze.

"Do you know I'm in love with you?"

"Not a good idea."

She turned her head forward, a consternated look on her face. "I know, but there you have it."

He didn't know what to say to that, so he said nothing.

He kept a sharp eye out for Bitterman or anyone else who might be on their trail. This was trouble country, for sure. That misery in his body from the day before made that all too clear. But they rode into the Comanche headquarters having encountered a grizzly climbing a forested ridge a good two hundreds distant, paying no attention to them.

"Good Lord—what in hell happened to you?" Garth Deveraux asked Nordic as he stood on the broad porch of his impressive mountain lodge. He gazed down at his daughter and his range rider with no little disapproval.

Alexandra swung down from her black and tossed the reins to one of the hostlers who'd followed her and Nordic to the lodge. As the hostler led the handsome gelding off to the stables, Alexandra said, "It was Half-Moon, Father."

The rancher frowned at Nordic. "Why?"

"I was in the wrong place at the wrong time."

Alexandra stared up at Nordic, placed her hand on his knee. "Thank you."

Anders nodded.

She climbed the porch steps and disappeared into the lodge.

Deveraux turned to Nordic. "Light and sit a spell. We have to palaver, as you Americans call it. We need to discuss this…whatever in God's name it is."

He turned to walk across the porch. Nordic stepped down from Apache's back, dropped his reins, and said to Finn sitting nearby, looking expectant. "Stay, boy."

He climbed the steps, crossed the porch, and followed Deveraux into the grand, log lodge. Deveraux traced a circuitous route between and through well-appointed rooms including two parlors, one with a grand piano, and a large dining room to his spacious office at the back. He had a fire going in the hearth. He told Nordic to take a seat, indicating an overstuffed leather chair by the fire, then fetched cigars and brandy and sat down in a matching leather chair on the other side of a small cherry wooden table from Nordic.

When they both had their cigars lit, smoke billowing around them, their brandy snifters on the table before them, Deveraux leaned back in his chair and eyed Nordic through the wafting smoke wreaths. The fire in the hearth crackled and popped, perfuming the book-lined office trimmed with trophy heads and large oil paintings Nordic assumed depicted the English countryside, all ensconced in the aromatic smell of pine and cedar.

"All right," Anders said after sipping his brandy, "let's have it."

"She is not to visit you anymore. She leaves early, even before I—an early riser—am up. She has long been in the habit of sneaking around behind my back, but I'm putting a stop to this here and now."

"Don't blame you."

"I fear she is in love with you."

"I do, too."

"Do you love her?"

"It wouldn't matter if I did. I know that."

"Good." Deveraux sipped his brandy, puffed his cigar. "Do you want me to send men to Half-Moon? I can drag Ehrlich out of there and—"

"And start a war over me?" Nordic chuckled. "I'm not worth it."

"You're problematic—I'll give you that. My foreman is missing a toe because of you. But you're effective on the range despite the beating you took."

"They had me outnumbered and one of them is likely in town having his jaw set as we speak."

Deveraux chuckled and took another sip of his brandy. "I like you, Nordic, but..." He wagged his head. "Are you fit enough to get back out on the range?"

"Yep."

The rancher grimaced. "That's got to hurt."

"I've endured worse."

Again, the rancher chuckled. "Don't doubt it a bit."

Anders finished his brandy and stubbed his cigar out in an ashtray. Rising and donning his hat, which he'd set on the stout arm of the leather chair, he said, "I best get back to it. I'll stiffen up if I sit too long."

"Watch for nesters. There are more from where the Nordstroms came."

Towering over the rancher still seated in his chair, Nordic said, "I'm not killing nesters."

"Don't worry—I'll have my men do it." Deveraux pointed an admonishing finger at his rider. "You stay out of it."

"I won't."

Deveraux merely grunted at that.

Nordic walked to the office door.

"Nordic?"

Anders turned around. The gray-headed but still powerfully built older man said, "Don't kill my fore-man. I know he, too, is problematic, but that's the kind of man I need to protect my holdings."

"I understand. But if he comes for me, you can bet he'll be returned here tied belly down across his saddle."

Deveraux hardened his jaws and cursed.

Nordic found his way back to the front of the house and went out to where Finn waited for him on the porch. He stepped into the saddle, said, "Come on, Finn," and started out.

As he crossed the ranch yard toward the mouth of the trail, he glanced up at the lodge's second story to see Alexandra watching him from her window.

————

I n her bedroom on the second story of the Deveraux ranch house, Alexandra stepped away from her window. Enraged, for she knew what her father had told Nordic, she clenched her fists at her sides then swung around suddenly and walked to her bedroom door. She stepped into the hall and strode quickly downstairs and to the rear of the house.

Her father's office door was open.

He sat with his back to her, sipping brandy and smoking a cigar.

"Come on in," Garth Deveraux said, taking another pull from the cigar. "I figured you'd be there soon."

"Damn right I'm here," Alexandra said, and strode into the office. She stopped near her father and glared down at him. "How dare you interfere in my life. I'm twenty-four!"

"Pour yourself a brandy."

She gave an agonized cry and strode to the liquor cabinet on the wall above which hung an oil painting of the Deveraux lodge. It was nearly twenty years old and had been painted by an artist her father had commissioned from London. Garth's pride and arrogance were second to none. She splashed brandy into a snifter, took a deep swallow, then replaced what she'd drunk from the decanter, and walked over and sat down across from her father, who, with a vaguely and irritatingly amused expression, smoked the cigar and sipped his brandy.

"You were saying?" he said.

Alexandra tried to keep her expression stony, but she knew her face was red. Inside, she was seething.

"I said, how dare you interfere in my life!"

"You're my daughter, and your life is mine to interfere with."

"What arrogance!"

"You are not to sneak out and ride to see the Dakotan ever again. That relationship is over."

"It's not over till I say it's over!"

Deveraux smiled coldly. "Like I said…"

"You told him to stay out of my life, didn't you?"

"You were eavesdropping, I take it?"

"I don't have to eavesdrop on you, Father. I know you well enough."

"Good. You will stay here where I can keep an eye on you from now on. Until I can find someone suited to your station. How do you think it would look to my fellow ranchers and business associates if they saw you cavorting with the likes of that big…big…rough-hewn nomad and his currish dog?"

Alexandra gave a wail of fury, leaped to her feet, and threw her snifter into the fire, where it shattered, the brandy steaming in the flames. She marched to the door.

"Alexandra!" Deveraux yelled. He'd always been

frustrated by his daughter's defiance, but now he was as angry as she was.

Alexandra left the room, marched through the house, and climbed the stairs. In her room she filled a carpetbag and headed back downstairs. Her father stood at the newel post.

"Where do you think you're going?"

She brushed past him. "Wherever I damn well please!"

Deveraux grabbed her arm. "I'll say you're not!"

She jerked her arm out of his hand. "Unhand me!"

She marched out of the house, across the yard, and into one of the ranch's three stables. Inside, the hostler, Chauncey Lewis, was forking morning feed to the stabled horses.

"Chauncey, saddle my sorrel!" she ordered.

Chauncey, a big man in overalls, looked at her dubiously. "Uh...well...all right, Miss Dev—"

Deveraux's deep voice thundered from the porch of the lodge. "Chauncey, you will saddle no horses for my daughter!"

Alexandra kept her eyes on the beefy, bearded hostler. "Saddle her. Chop-chop!"

"Chauncey, if you saddle a horse for her, you're fired!"

Chauncey's big face gained a truly agonized expression. "Ah, now, Miss Deveraux—you know I can't go against your—"

Alexandra dropped the carpetbag and stormed toward the stall in which her sorrel mare resided, poking her head over the door and regarding her stormy master with a puzzled expression.

A few minutes later, Alexandra and the sorrel, the young woman's carpetbag hanging from the saddle horn, galloped out of the barn and swung a hard left.

Deveraux was striding toward her from the lodge, his face red and swollen with rage. "Alexandra—I strictly forbid you!"

"I'm going to spend a few days in town!" Alexandra shouted back over her shoulder as the sorrel galloped toward the mouth of the trail. "I need to be anywhere but here…with *you*!"

CHAPTER SEVENTEEN

With a wild fury, Alexandra galloped along the twisting, turning Avalanche Creek, heading north toward the canyon of the Cache la Poudre River, the trail along which would take her to town. After a few minutes of hard riding, she rode around a bend in the trail and found four men on horseback, facing her, blocking her way.

Alexandra checked down the sorrel and curveted the mount, staring at the four—one of whom had a white cloth knotted under chin. It ran up and over the top of his head, beneath his hat. It was holding his jaw in place.

"Uh-oh," Alexandra said.

All four men stared at her with open menace in their hard eyes.

She froze in terror. They were Half-Moon riders.

They all glanced at each other and then the oldest of the bunch said, "That's Deveraux's princess!"

They spurred their horses into leaping gallops,

whooping and hollering like crazed coyotes on the blood scent.

"Oh, god! Oh, god!"

Alexandra reined the sorrel around, but her assailants were already on her. The older man, whom Alexandra knew was "Big" Louis Kyle, swept an arm around her and pulled her off the sorrel's back. He laughed and whooped and reined his dun off the trail and into the brush. He threw Alexandra to the ground and rolled her onto her back. He leaped on top of her, raking his hands all over her. The stench of the whisky he'd likely been chugging all night filled her nose along with his sweat stench and almost made her vomit.

As the other three younger men gathered around Big Louis and Alexandra, cheering, he lifted her skirt up and pulled down her bloomers, exposing her to the group.

The younger men cheered louder.

Alexandra screamed.

———

Nordic reined Apache to an abrupt halt.

The scream he'd just heard echoed around the ridges.

It came from below him on his left, from Poudre Canyon maybe a half mile down the ridge. He was riding the long way to the cabin to check out a cabin near here often used by cattle rustlers. He tried to keep it cleaned out because the outlaws who used it were like a catchy disease—if they were not expunged, they could infect the entire Never Summer Range.

The scream again. Nordic recognized it.

It was Alexandra.

He reined Apache hard left, yelled, "Come on, Finn!" Horse, rider, and dog dropped down the steep forest ridge to the canyon below. He heard men yelling and a woman shouting curses.

He rode hard down the canyon.

He saw the men grouped around Alexandra, who was trying to hold them off with a stout branch. One of the men was down and writhing, holding his privates. Nordic unholstered his .44, cocked it, and aimed straight out from his shoulder. The three men circling Alexandra just now heard the thundering hooves of Nordic's Appaloosa and swung around, drawing their own revolvers.

Anders's pistol roared once...twice...three times.

Finn barked angrily.

Two of the men screamed and dropped. The third twisted around, his pistol in his hand. He gave a shrill curse, then Nordic shot him in the back of the head.

Alexandra stared at him in shock, her blouse open, hair and skirt disheveled.

She glanced at the writhing man on the ground, holding his bleeding right ear.

She apparently beaned him good with the branch. He was the stout older man who'd been with the other three the day before. He'd assaulted Anders mercilessly. Nordic moved Apache over to him and looked down at him.

The older man glanced up at Anders. Fear glazed his eyes along with the pain of Alexandra's braining.

"No," he pleaded. "No...*please*...!"

Anders drilled a round through the dead center of his forehead.

Anders turned to Alexandra. She still held the branch like a club, her eyes wide and round with terror. Now, slowly, she lowered it, slid her gaze from the dead man near Apache to Anders. Tears glazed her eyes. She dropped the branch and sobbed.

Nordic dismounted and hurried over to her, as did Finn, yipping his concern.

She threw her arms around him and sobbed against his neck. She clung to him as though he were a raft in angry waters.

"My god," she rasped. "What are you doing out here?"

"Just happened to be in the right place at the right time, I reckon." Anders pushed her away from him, stared down at her tear-streaked face. "What are *you* doin' out here?"

She sniffed and rubbed tears from her cheeks with the backs of her hands. "Father and I... We got into a terrible fight. I'm going to town for a few days. I can't stand the sight of him!"

"Don't do that, Alexandra. He needs you an' you need him."

"You don't understand. I've never been in love before."

Nordic shook his head. He never should have

kissed her. "Alex, forget about me. I'm wayyy beneath you."

"You're in love with me, too," she said, dipping her chin and looking up at him beneath her brows, her eyes narrowed. "I know you are!"

Sitting at their feet, Finn barked and glanced up at Anders, tilting his head and mewling softly.

"He knows it, too," Alexandra said.

"It doesn't matter, Alex. It just doesn't matter. I'm not *that* kind of man. Never have been. Never will be."

She turned her mouth corners down and nodded. "I know."

She turned away from him, saw her sorrel standing up trail fifty yards, the outlaws' horses gathered around him, idly grazing. The sorrel watched Alexandra with her ears pricked curiously. Alexandra picked up her hat, set it on her head, and started walking toward the waiting horse.

Anders said, "Alex. Go home. There are more men in these mountains just like these."

She said nothing. She grabbed her sorrel's reins and stepped into the leather. She glanced at Anders once more then reined the mare around and pressed the heels of her boots against the horse's loins, and they started trotting up trail, Alexandra's hair bouncing on her shoulders. She climbed a rocky rise and disappeared down the opposite side.

Nordic sighed.

Finn stared up at him, softly yipping.

"I know, boy." He reached down to give his friend's head a single pat. "I know…"

He mounted, and Apache and Nordic and Finn headed down trail, in the opposite direction of the young woman he hated himself for loving...hated her for loving him.

He didn't know he was being watched from some shrubs near where the dead men lay.

———

C lem Coffee crouched, peering through a clump of cedars until the big man from Dakota disappeared to the south.

Coffee's heart was pounding. His eyes were wide. Sweat streaked his cheeks.

He was tall and thin, and he wore a soup-strainer mustache. He was in his late fifties and knew his boss and owner of the Half-Moon would lay him on the chopping block soon, for the aging Coffee was having trouble keeping up with the other riders. That was why he was near when he heard the girl's screams and rode over to investigate just as the big man from Dakota and his dog rode in, and the big man gunned down Skinner, Pepper, Delaney, and Big Louis Kyle. Shot them like he was shooting coyotes off a calf!

"Oh...oh...oh," Coffee said, rubbing his hands together, grinning. "Oh lordy...wait till the boss hears about this!"

He turned and strode off into the forest, climbed a low rise, dropping down the other side, moving so fast he tripped over his own feet and nearly fell three times. His steeldust gelding stood at the bottom of the rise, tied to a gnarled cedar jutting up beside a large rock.

Chuckling to himself, he untied the reins and climbed into the saddle, wincing at the aches in his aging hips. They'd been battered over the past forty years from his stint as a horsebreaker when he was younger to saloon and bunkhouse brawls and tumbles from his horse when he'd gone head-to-head with an angry bull or a heifer believing she was protecting her calf.

It had been a long, hard career—the cowboy life.

But Coffee wasn't ready to give it up yet. What else could he do? He knew no other way of life. He wasn't ready to sit in some stale-smelling room in a house of Christian charity, rolling cigarettes and taking sips from a forbidden bottle of Who-Hit-John.

He put the steeldust into a dead run in the direction of the Half-Moon headquarters, five miles away.

He came to the trail that led to the Half-Moon, swung west, and, slowing the steeldust to rest him for five minutes then spurring the gelding into a gallop once more. He passed through the Half-Moon's portal an hour after he'd left the dead Half-Moon riders. He galloped past the log barn and hitch-and-rail corrals, the men working in the corrals eyeing him speculatively.

He reined up in front of his boss's long, low, log, shake-shingle shack as one of the men from the corral yelled, "Coffee's here, boss—ridin' like he's got a grizz on his tail!"

The others laughed.

The shack's rickety door opened, and a short, big-gutted man stepped onto the worn front porch, wearing a ratty robe over wash-worn longhandles, elk hide slippers on his feet. His face wore a week's worth of steel-gray stubble. His thin hair was mussed. A loosely rolled cigarette drooped from his thin-lipped mouth. Coffee could smell the liquor on the man's lips from where he sat the steeldust just off the humble shack, which, like the boss—Frank Ehrlich—himself, had known much better days.

Ehrlich scowled at the oldest rider on his roll and said around the cigarette in his mouth, "What in hell are you doin', Coffee? You tryin' to kill that hoss?"

The steeldust's neck was lathered with silver sweat.

Coffee drew a deep breath and gave his head a single shake. Breathless, he said, "Got news, boss. Big news. *Bad* news!"

Ashes dripped from the rancher's cigarette as he continued scowling impatiently at Coffee. "All right, all right. What do you say you get your bloomers out of a twist and give me the *big, bad* news!"

The men around the corrals laughed.

"S-Skinner, Pepper, Delaney, an' *Big Louis*… they're all *dead*! Gunned down in cold blood by the Nordic…that big fella from Dakota workin' for Garth Deveraux!"

A hush fell over the corrals.

The rancher studied Coffee skeptically. "The Nordic…he killed those men? They was supposed to be at the North Gate graze, movin'…"

"Well, they didn't make it. They're lyin' dead along the trail, sorta near the base of Elephant Peak!"

"Why?"

"There weren't no good reason. They was just funnin' with Deveraux's daughter is all. Of course, she weren't goin' along with it. That's an uppity one there! In fact, she took her stout branch and rammed it over Big Louis's head. When the others seen that, they went after her. She fended 'em off with the club while poor Louis lay on the ground. She prob'ly busted his head. Blood was runnin' from his ear. Then the big Nordic fella rode in an' shot 'em all...deader'n posts!"

Frank Ehrlich studied on that for a bit then drew on his quirley and let the smoke out through his wedge-shaped nose. "He did, did he?"

"Yessir!"

"What'd you do to help?"

"What's...what's that...?"

"What'd you do to help?!"

That rocked Coffee back on his proverbial heels. "Well, uh...there weren't much I could do against the Nordic..."

"Because you're too damn old. And you're a damn coward!"

"No, sir, boss...no, sir. I thought I should just go fer help is all. He'd have just shot me dead an' nobody woulda...you know...knew it happened."

"Where's the girl now?"

"She, uh...told the Nordic she was goin' to town." Coffee narrowed an eye and smiled with amusement. "She an' the big fella...they got somethin' goin'."

"Oh, they do, do they?"

"Yessir!"

"Where's the Nordic now?"

"Well, uh…he rode west after she rode east toward Camp Collins."

"You damn fool," Ehrlich said, his pudgy, round face swelling with anger. "You coulda shot him yourself. I take it you were hidden, peering like a peeping tom. You coulda shot him right out of his damn saddle an' it all woulda been takin' care of!"

Coffee opened his mouth to speak but no words came out.

Ehrlich looked toward the corrals and said, "Johnson, Sawchuck—get your asses over here!"

When the two men came running to stand near Coffee in the saddle, Ehrlich said, "Johnson and Sawchuck. I want you to scour the mountains for that Nordic. It's high time he stopped ridin' like he owned every spread in the Never Summers, carryin' himself like he's some big mucky-muck. I want his head brought back to me in a gunnysack. Then I want you to kill Deveraux. I don't care how you do it—I just want it done!"

"Just us, boss?"

"It'll only take three if you're good enough. Too many, an' you invite suspicion. Johnson, you know where Deveraux's line shacks are, don't you?"

The man called Johnson—of medium height and long-haired, a hooked scar on his cheek—said, "You bet. Seen 'em all at roundup, think I know which one the Nordic is holed up in. Won't be easy…"

"Life ain't easy."

Johnson frowned suddenly, curious. "Who's the third one?"

"Coffee."

Coffee looked astounded. "What's that, boss?"

"You're gonna help track down that Nordic and the too-big-fer-his-britches Deveraux and kill 'em. When you've killed the Nordic, ride into Deveraux's headquarters, say you need a word about the herds. There won't be many men around during the day. Shoot him out of his boots!"

Bing Johnson and Merle Sawchuck looked skeptically at the tongue-tied Coffee, then swung around and headed for the stables, muttering to each other.

Ehrlich said to Coffee, "Well, don't just stand there like a lump on a log. Ride to the stable and switch out your hoss!"

When Coffee had ridden slowly, haltingly toward the stables, Ehrlich turned to the corral again, and yelled, "Landry! Cortez! Get over here." He grinned and blew more smoke out his nose. "I gotta special job for you in town…"

CHAPTER EIGHTEEN

Alexandra rode into Camp Collins ninety minutes later, still shaking not only from her encounter with the Half-Moon men but her encounter with her father, too. She had an odd and terrifying feeling that she was no longer the person she'd woken up as.

Something very significant was going to change in her life.

She didn't think she'd be in the Never Summers much longer. She had to be independent. She had to be her own woman who made her own decisions. They couldn't be left to a man like Garth Deveraux, nor to a man like Anders Nordic, either, for that matter.

She rode down the wide, dusty main street, not seeing much but sensing men turning toward her with typical male interest. She was just passing the Long-mont Saloon when she heard a man say, "Well, lookee here…if it ain't Deveraux's princess!"

"Yeah," said another man, "her highness her ownself…"

Alexandra reined the sorrel to a halt. A man driving a big lumber dray behind her cursed and pulled his team around her, giving her an angry look. "Look, miss," he said, scowling at her, "I know who you are an' all, but you don't own the street!"

Alexandra ignored him. Her attention was on one of the five men gathered on the boardwalk fronting the Longmont Saloon. Each had a soapy beer mug in his gloved fist. Alexandra reined the sorrel over and stopped before the men, between two hitchracks to which a half dozen saddled horses were tied.

She stared at a seedy-eyed blond man in a black hat wearing a thick, sandy-blond mustache. He was somewhere in his early twenties—a cowboy from one of the near ranches. He wore a soiled, red, neck-knotted bandanna. "What did you call me?" Alexandra asked, keeping her voice bland.

But her eyes were hard. She was tired of men, and she wasn't about to take any more from such as these, especially.

The skin above the bridge of the man's nose wrinkled. A leering grin shaped itself on his lips beneath the mustache. "What's that…Princess Deveraux?"

He glanced at the others who joined him in the amusement, chuckling.

One of the others said, "I think ya got her mad, Ten!"

The others laughed.

Alexandra calmly pulled the .44 from the holster

she'd strapped to her saddle horn after her encounter with the Half-Moon men, ratcheted the hammer back, and aimed at the blond man. His eyes widened with sudden fear, and he raised his hands, palms out.

"Now, no…*wait*!"

Alexandra lowered the barrel a little. The .44 thundered. The blond gent yelped and leaped a foot in the air as the bullet drilled a slivery hole between his boots. Alexandra recocked the .44 and aimed a little high but not by much.

She narrowed one eye and said, "If you ever call me anything but Miss Deveraux, you'll be singing soprano. Do I make myself clear?"

The man just gaped at her, terror still in his eyes.

"Don't make me repeat the question, you cowardly tinhorn."

"Yeah, yeah, yeah!" the tinhorn said. "You made yourself clear, uh…Miss Deveraux!"

The others stared at her now with much the same expression as the tinhorn.

"Good." Alexandra returned the .44 to its holster on the right side of her saddle and reined the sorrel away from the stunned drovers. When she was ten feet away, she heard one of them break his silence to chuckle and say, mockingly, "Yeah, yeah, yeah, you made yourself clear, uh…Miss Deveraux!"

He and the others laughed.

Alexandra smiled as she put the sorrel up to one of the three hitchracks fronting the Dancing Bear Saloon a block away from and on the other side of the street from the Longmont and the five cowboys. She went into the tony hotel and saloon—at least, tony for these parts—and ordered a room. She paid the old man in a green eyeshade sitting behind the desk twenty-five cents to have the sorrel taken over to the High-Country Livery and Feed Barn, ordered a hot bath with plenty of soap and towels, a bottle of whisky, and climbed the stairs to her third-story room.

A half hour later she sat in the hot, soapy water, a bottle and a whisky glass on a chair beside the tub, lounging back in the water and, rubbing her feet soothingly against the copper tub's far end.

She sipped the whisky and smiled. "I rather like being called a princess."

She took another sip of the whisky and, chuckling, pulled her head beneath the water.

———

Neil Landry and Ortego Cortez rode into Camp Collins in the late afternoon, swinging their heads left and right, scouring the boardwalks for the pretty Deveraux girl, whom they'd been ordered to shoot so full of lead she'd rattle when she walked. That had amused both men. They'd seen the uppity woman on the range several times, riding one of her string of blooded horses and not favoring them with a single passing glance.

They'd once watched her swim in a backwater pool of Avalanche Creek, which she'd thought was private, and, elbowing each other, both had drooled and felt the goatish itch all over their bodies.

Landry was a short but deadly shootist from Texas. He had coal-black hair, one cobalt wandering eye, and muttonchop coal-black side whiskers. He wore two .45s on his hips and dressed all in black save a billowy red neckerchief.

Ortego Cortez was also a gunfighter who hailed from southern Sonora. As a boy he'd been kidnapped by Yaqui, who'd intended to enslave him in their gold mines, but he'd shot his way out and headed north. He was primarily a cowpuncher, but he knew his way around a six-shooter, as well. He'd killed several men in saloons across Arizona and New Mexico. He was here in the Never Summers cooling his heels after one of the men he'd killed only months ago had turned out to be a deputy US marshal.

He wore a perpetual, leering grin on his broad mouth trimmed with mare's tail mustaches that hung six inches down from both corners of his mouth.

He wore it now, swinging his head from side to side, looking for Deveraux's gringo beauty, the image of whom, naked, had blazed itself on his lusty brain. The only reason he and Landry hadn't ravaged her was because there was something mysterious and untouchable about her.

Still, she'd been mighty fun to look at. *Dios mio!*

When they were halfway through town, still busy in the later afternoon, Landry turned to Cortez and canted his head to the right, indicating the Longmont Saloon at the hitchracks of which a good dozen horses were tied. They knew several drovers who patronized the place—the kind of men who would know, rather by personal observation or word-of-mouth, where the pretty Deveraux goddess had headed for in town.

They each put their horses up to a crowded hitchrack, swung down, and looped their reins around their respective racks. They mounted the boardwalk, hearing the roar of conversation inside the seedy but popular watering hole, spurs chinging on the worn floorboards, and pushed through the batwings.

They made their way through the crowd and bellied up to the bar, to the right of men from the Long's Peak Spread and ordered whisky shots. They ordered them for the five men to their right, as well, and Landry asked Dub Smith, "You see the Deveraux princess in town today?"

Smith had just taken a sip of his drink and now he sprayed it out of his mouth and across the bar, laughing. "Oh, yeah!" he said. "But I wouldn't call her 'princess' to her face, if I were you! Ten Siegel's lucky he still has the equipment he's gonna need later tonight!"

"What's that? What's that?" asked the man standing to the right of Dub Smith.

Smith turned to him and said, "They're lookin' fer the princess."

"Oh, man!" the second man said, glancing fearfully toward the batwings. "Don't call her that. If'n you seen what she did to me...!"

Smith and the two men beyond the second man laughed.

The second man threw back an entire shot of whisky.

"You fellas know where she is?" asked Cortez.

Smith shrugged.

"Oh, I know. I seen her ride over to the Dancin' Bear. Must be plannin' on spendin' the night in town. Means I'll be ridin' out at sundown. Ain't spendin' a night in town with that polecat!"

Landry and Cortez shared a glance.

Cortez said, "We might as well have a few drinks here…a few drinks there."

"A little liquid courage?" said Landry.

Both men laughed and ordered a beer and more whisky.

———

Alexandra was so exhausted from the doings of the day as well as the whisky, she fell asleep in the bathtub.

When she woke, she saw through the room's two windows that the sun was impaled on the tip of one of the tall peaks of the Never Summers west of town. No wonder she was hungry.

She toweled off, dried her hair the best she could, combed it out, and dressed in the outfit she'd packed in her carpetbag—a fresh, dark wool skirt, white blouse under a black vest, and wide black belt with a gold buckle. She took another swig from the whisky bottle then headed down the carpeted hall, down the broad carpeted stairs with its varnished oak railing, to the dining room and drinking hall below. An ornate bar flanked by a polished backbar mirror lay at the room's far end. The three bartenders, dressed in pinstripe shirts and bow ties, comb marks showing in their pomaded hair, were serving drinks to the ten or so cowboys and well-dressed businessmen standing at the bar.

Waiters in similar costumes and with clean, white aprons tied around their waists hauled out sizzling steaks or cuts of roast beef or elk medallions out of the kitchen flanking the bar. There were another ten or so diners. On the weekends this place usually filled and the tobacco smoke was so thick you couldn't see across the room. But this was a weeknight, and the room was nicely sedate.

Alexandra had come here to rest and relax in peace and quiet, with good food and good hooch. She knew she could get a decent Scotch here...after a big, succulent T-bone, baked potato, and a side of greens.

She sat at an isolated table near the staircase and at the room's rear. All heads had turned to her. Mutters rose. Few women patronized saloons alone. Of course, there was the breed of female who didn't patronize them at all. How scandalous! Alexandra loved a good saloon and, like her father, enjoyed a good brand of strong drink. A waiter she knew well—Herman Lochlin—who was middle-aged, gray-haired, and carried himself with an elegant air, approached her table holding an empty tray shoulder high.

"Hello, Miss Deveraux. Welcome, welcome. Nice to see you again. On a vacation from school?"

"To be honest with you, Herman, I'm not sure what I'm doing. I rode to town to possibly figure that out. In the meantime, I'll order the usual. A double shot of good Scotch first, however."

She hoped he'd remember what her "usual" was. She hadn't been here since she'd last visited her home country.

He gave her a cordial bow and retreated to the kitchen.

He returned a few minutes later with a liberal portion of Scotch in a cut glass crystal goblet. Alexandria gave him a warm smile. He returned it with a wink and headed back to the bar to fill another drink order.

She leaned forward, elbows on the table, holding the glass in her hand, pensively sipping her Scotch. Her heart was heavy. A depression weighed on her heavily. She was still shaken from her encounter with the savage Half-Moon men.

What would have happened if Nordic hadn't come to her rescue?

She knew very well.

She gave a shudder.

Nordic.

Why had she fallen in love with a man she couldn't have? That wasn't for her father to decide. She might have fooled herself into believing she could have him, but that was silly thinking, she knew now. Had known since yesterday.

She felt foolish and heartbroken at the same time.

When Herman came with her sizzling steak on one big platter and a baked potato and corn on another platter, garnished with a dill pickle, she ordered another Scotch.

Herman smiled. "Father trouble?"

"Always."

He nodded sagely, fetched the Scotch, and resumed taking orders.

Quite a few other customers had come in and sat down or bellied up to the bar since she'd taken her own private seat. She didn't look at them. She was too busy cutting the succulent T-bone and sipping the Scotch. She also didn't want to see them regarding her skeptically, wondering, as always, what the pretty Deveraux girl was doing in town alone.

But then, she usually came alone, though her father, of course, disapproved. After her encounter with the Half-Moon savages, she might think it through a little better next time. Might, at least, wear her gun on her saddle, where she could reach for it quickly and make any man accosting her pay dearly for his goatishness.

She remembered the leers on the Half-Moon riders' faces. Then she remembered their womanish screams as Anders cut them down with his Colt .44. She was drunk enough to chuckle aloud at that, as she cut into the last third of her steak. She didn't care who heard. She didn't care who thought she should be locked in an asylum. Maybe she should be. She knew for one thing that she was far different from the young women she'd known in school back East.

Everyone could go to hell.

Again, she chuckled and, having eaten all she could and ready to repair to her room with more Scotch, wiped her mouth with her burgundy cloth napkin. As she did, she looked toward the bar. Her gaze settled on two men sitting near it. Both were looking over their shoulders at her. One was a long-haired white man. Rather uncouth looking. Not like anyone else who patronizes the Dancing Bear. The other was a short, curly-haired Mexican with long, dark brown mustaches.

When they saw her returning their gazes, they quickly turned away. The Mexican refilled their shot glasses from a bottle on their table. They had a definite look of trouble about them.

Who were they?

She'd seen them before in the Never Summers. Range riders.

For whom?

The Half-Moon?

Had someone seen Nordic blow the Half-Moon riders who'd accosted her out of their boots? As far as she knew, no one else but her, the would-be rapists, and Nordic had been in the area when the shootings had occurred. If someone had reported back to the savage Frank Ehrlich, part-time rancher and full-time alcoholic, not only would she likely be in trouble, but Anders would, too.

Maybe those two were just ogling her along with the other men in the room.

She hoped that was true. But she had an uneasy feeling and just wanted to secure another bottle to calm her nerves and to return to her room. She was glad she had a stout .44 up there—one, when she'd started filling out and becoming a woman, her father had taught her to shoot. It was no lady's pistol. No derringer.

It was a man's gun, one which her right arm and hand had become strong enough to hold and to shoot true...

She ordered a bottle from Herman and rose from her chair.

She glanced into the backbar mirror. The two men were watching her movements there. She turned away from them quickly and, cradling the bottle like a baby, hurried to the stairs. She used her key to open her door, stepped in, closed the door, and locked it. She stood facing the door and sighed.

Her heart slowed.

She sat at a table, poured herself a drink, and sipped it slowly, trying to think no longer about the trying day. The trouble that may have followed her out of the mountains.

No, she was just being overly emotional. Those men had just been admiring her filled blouse.

Men.

Didn't they all need to be gutshot and thrown in a ravine?

She laughed and choked on the Scotch. She leaned forward against the table, chuckling and massaging her temples.

Alexandra, why in hell did you come back here? The men here were trouble. Even her father's men.

She thought of Wayne Bitterman and shuddered, took another big swallow of the top-shelf Scotch.

She sat sipping the hooch, tired of being frightened.

Gradually, anger came in to shove away the fear.

She heard men passing in the hall—laughing, cajoling horse and beef buyers, mostly. After midnight, the hotel went silent…save for another set of footsteps in the hall.

There was a furtive air about these.

She heard whispering.

The footsteps stopped outside her door.

Alexandra went to the door, unlocked it, and opened it.

The hangdog man with one wandering eye and the snickering, curly Mexican stood facing her, their pistols held straight down by their sides.

"Kind of late for a visit—isn't it, gentleman?" Alexandra gave a frigid smile. "I use that term very loosely."

Both men's lower jaws dropped.

The Mexican stopped snickering.

They'd just started to raise their pistols, yelling, when Alexandra shot both in the face.

They piled up atop each other against the hall's opposite wall, shuddering.

Alexandra lowered the .44 and closed the door.

Men…

At long last, time for bed.

CHAPTER NINETEEN

An hour after he'd shot the Half-Moon men, Nordic rode into the Comanche Ranch head-quarters sitting atop the pine-clad mountain it had been named after. Finn had disappeared a few times after they'd left the dead Half-Moon riders. He'd run off to chase rabbits, but he was close on Apache's heels now, panting.

There were a few Comanche men working horses in the corral. They all turned their heads to give Nordic the woolly eyeball as he approached the big lodge. One of the men sitting on the corral, watching two others work still-green mustangs, twisted around toward the lodge, cupped his hands around his mouth, and yelled, "Visitor, boss! The big bastard from Dakota!"

The others laughed.

Nordic shook his head and grinned. Always nice to be liked.

The big oak door on the far side of the porch

opened. Deveraux walked to the top of the steps, scowling and hooking his thumbs behind his wide, brown belt with a big, square, brass buckle, and said in his thick British brogue, "Did you see my daughter out there?"

"Yep."

Garth Deveraux hardened his jaws and cursed.

"It ain't what you think."

Deveraux let the air out of his puffed-up chest. He beckoned brusquely. "Come in. I have coffee on the range."

Nordic wanted to get back to Sarah and Robert at the cabin. He thought they were safe, however. Bitterman knew what would happen to him if he touched a hair on their heads. He knew it wouldn't be pretty, and it wouldn't be fast, either.

Besides, he couldn't discuss what had happened on the trail with Deveraux from horseback. They both needed to be sitting down for this.

He swung down from Apache's back, tossed the reins over the hitchrack, told Finn to stay, and mounted the porch steps. Deveraux had left the door open. He found the rancher in the kitchen off the foyer to the left, filling two stone mugs on an oilcloth covered table from a big, black pot. Steam wafted up around his big, gray, leonine head.

He shoved one of the mugs to the opposite side of the table and, returning the pot to the range, said, "Have a seat."

Nordic sat down. He removed his hat and gloves, set them on the chair to his left, and took the hot mug in his hands. Deveraux sat across from him. He looked older than he had the last time Anders had seen him. His eyes were dull, his otherwise Indian-dark cheeks mottled pale. They'd had a good fight, all right. Him and his strong-willed daughter.

Nordic just wished it hadn't involved him. There'd been no point in that. He didn't care to get mixed up in personal business. That was why he lived the life he lived—moving from one remote line shack to another. Avoiding people.

Deveraux sighed, picked up his mug, blew on the coffee, and sipped.

He set the cup down. "All right, spill it. What happened between you and Alexandra?"

"You're not gonna like it."

The angry scowl returned to the older man's face.

"Nothin' like that," Nordic said. "I was gonna check out that old line shack on open range northwest of here when I heard a scream. It was Alexandra."

"What?"

Anders held up a hand, palm out. "When I rode up, she was fending off four Half-Moon riders with a tree branch. They were the same four who made me look pretty. She clubbed one pretty good and he was down with a bloody ear and probably a cracked skull. Better than what he deserved. The others were moving in on her. I shot them. They're likely bein' given shovels by Ol' Scratch even as we speak."

"Half-Moon riders." Deveraux flared his nostrils. "That damn Frank Ehrlich!"

"Thought you should know."

Deveraux slapped the table. "Of course, I should know!"

"About Alexandra, of course. But three of Ehrlich's men are dead and it happened close to Comanche range. He might place the blame on you."

"What'd you do with the bodies?"

"Left them near the trail." Nordic shrugged. "No point in tryin' to hide them. Ehrlich's gonna know they're gone and suspect what happened to 'em, though he probably won't know the circumstances, unless…"

"Unless what?"

Nordic took another sip of his coffee and shook his head. "I don't know. I just had the sense someone else might have been there. I looked around, didn't see anyone. I figure if another Half-Moon rider was out there, he'd have come to help his pards."

"You should have disposed of the bodies."

"Waste of time. Ehrlich will likely figure it was me. I'm responsible for the most deaths in these mountains over the past few months. He'll come for me first, possibly you second. Just keep your guard up and a few men around the place."

Deveraux winced and took another sip of his coffee. "A war has been brewin' between me and Ehrlich for a long time. Maybe it's time to get it over with." He looked at Nordic. "How is she?"

"Tough as ever. She went to town. I wanted her to go home, but of course she wouldn't listen."

"No, she wouldn't come back to me. She hates

me." Deveraux gave Anders a hard, direct look. "Over you."

Nordic sighed, scratched his brow. "She doesn't see it how it is."

"Did you kiss her?"

"Yes."

"I should fetch a big Colt and drill you through the heart!"

"I would if I were you."

Deveraux drew a deep breath. "Kind of hard to resist, though—isn't she?"

"Yep."

"I hate the way men look at her. Always have since she was twelve years old. Never had this kind of trouble, though. She seemed to have no interest in anything but her piano, cats, and horses. She once had two pet bobcats she raised when their mother was killed. Had a pet crow." Deveraux gave a wry chuff and shook his head. "Damn peculiar child. You know, I was a little worried about her. Figured she'd be married by now."

"But not to a man like me."

"Hell no!"

"I'm the last man she needs."

"I wanted her to marry the son of one of my business associates. Had two good ones picked out for her. I had them all out here for dinner with me and Alex. Hired a chef from Denver. She was nearly bored to tears. Left the table early to tend her pet muskrat!" Deveraux laughed and shook his head. "And then she falls for you."

It was Anders's turn to shake his head. "Nothin' seems to make sense sometimes." He finished his coffee and set the empty mug on the table. "Let me ask you a question. Does anyone in these mountains know where the line shack is? The one I'm in?"

"Oh, I'm sure a few have stumbled on it. I rode up there a few years ago and it looked like it had been occupied for a time. Probably by outlaws on the run."

"So, someone on the Half-Moon might know where it is."

"Possible. Watch your back."

Nordic rose. "Thanks for the coffee." He set his hat on his head and pulled on his gloves. "What's gonna happen with you and Alex?"

"Just like always, I have no idea. I've never wanted her to ride to town alone, but do you think that's ever stopped her?" Deveraux pursed his lips and shook his head. "Reads the craziest damn books. She's always riding some-damn-where I don't want her to go. To the Crags, for instance. Swims with her horse in Lake Agnes at the base of that formation. That place is teeming with outlaws. She's not afraid. She thinks her pistol will save her. She loves the Crags. Says she has a 'spiritual connection.' I suspect that's what she believes about you."

"You could have a worse daughter, Deveraux."

"She worries me."

"I hear they all worry their fathers. That's why I don't have any." Nordic pinched his hat brim to the man, left the kitchen, headed outside, and mounted Apache.

"Come on, Finn!"

The dog barked, eager to get moving again.

Anders booted the Appaloosa back down the mountain.

———

An hour later, climbing a forested ridge, a man's shrill laugh reached his ears.

"Whoa, whoa, whoa, boy," he said, reining Apache to a halt.

He turned his head to one side, pricking his ears.

Another laugh sounded and then a girl's scream came caroming from the direction of the line shack.

Finn barked and growled.

"Ah, hell!" Anders ground his heels into the Appaloosa's loins. The stallion leaped off its rear hooves and shot up and over the top of the ridge. More men's crazy laughter. Sarah screamed again.

Again, Finn barked.

Nordic cursed and urged the Appy into even more speed. Fifteen minutes later, the line shack came into view on the hill above the creek. Men were riding around the shack, yelling and howling like moon-crazed coyotes. There were three of them. Nordic recognized a couple as Half-Moon riders he'd seen on the open range. Sarah must be in the cabin, likely with the locking bar over the door.

Anders shucked his Yellowboy from its saddle sheath and cocked it one-handed.

One turned his head, saw Nordic galloping toward

them hell for leather, and cursed loudly. Finn was close on the Appy's heels. "The Nordic's comin', boys, an' he's got us flanked! Ride for it!"

All three rode around the side of the cabin toward the back, another man cursing, one horse whinnying shrilly. In seconds they were out of sight.

Nordic approached the cabin at a dead run, skidded the Appy to a stop, and leaped out of the saddle.

"Sarah!" he yelled, pounding on the door. "Are you all right?"

The baby was screaming.

"Anders!" Sarah cried.

The locking bar scraped out of its bracket, clattered onto the floor. She opened the door and stood holding the wailing little Robert in her arms. She was sobbing, tears streaking her cheeks.

"They rode up when I was out getting water. Scared me to death. I barely got back inside before they leaped out of their saddles and ran toward me."

"I'm going after them!"

Then Anders was back in the saddle and he, Apache, and Finn were running around the side of the cabin. Through the pines and firs, he saw the horseback riders galloping up the ridge behind the shack.

He booted the stallion up the ridge behind the stable, Finn running and growling behind him. The marauders rode up and over the top of the ridge, galloping down the opposite side. Apache traced a circuitous route through the forested side of the ridge. He rode up and over the top and started down the other side. He saw the riders ride into the forest and disappear.

Nordic slowed the stallion, not wanting to get caught in bushwhack.

Finn ran ahead until Anders said, "Hold on, Finn. We don't want to get caught in a lead storm!"

Nordic checked Apache down, stepped out of the leather and, holding the rifle up high across his chest, moving slowly down the ridge and quartering to his left. Finn was right behind him, panting. At the bottom of the ridge, he slowly approached the edge of the ravine. When he was twenty feet away, he got down on his hands and knees and told Finn to stay.

"You ain't armed, boy."

The dog sat down near the edge of the ravine and gave a low, disgruntled yip.

Staying low to the ground, Nordic doffed his *sombrero*, set it beside him on the ground, and edged a look over the lip of the ravine and to his right, where he'd seen the riders enter the wash. The wash twisted and curved. Several side canyons angled off its far side. A thin ribbon of a creek slid slowly through it, following the twisting bed.

Fresh horse tracks shown in the soft sand along both sides of the freshet.

Nordic donned his hat and slipped into the cut, holding his rifle straight out from his right hip. He looked around carefully then slowly started following the tracks of the three horses. When he'd walked thirty yards, the tracks swerved into a side canyon on his left. He followed them, staying close to the cut's left, eroded wall. The cut swerved off to the right around a bulge in the right wall.

He'd just moved around the bulge when a bullet whistled just inches off his right ear and slammed into the chalky wall behind him. He raised the Winchester and fired three quick rounds toward where he saw a hat crown around which powder smoke wafted. The shooter screamed and disappeared. Nordic stepped around the bulge in the canyon just as two more bullets whistled past him before slamming into the bulge where he'd been standing seconds before.

The other two shooters were holed up before a large rock on the ridge near where the first shooter had fired from. Two more shots came, powder smoke wafting up from behind the rock.

Anders said, "Here goes nothin'!" and ran out from behind the bulge toward the base of the ridge the two shooters were on. There was a slight shelf six feet from the base of the ridge. He crouched beneath it and waited, holding the Yellowboy straight up before him.

A long five minutes passed. Then a man shouted from above him, "Hey, Dakota, we know you're down there! Come on out an' show yourself. Let's get this over with!"

Nordic said nothing.

Another five minutes passed.

Then another.

Anders peered up around the shelf just above him.

He waited.

Sand and pebbles dribbled down over the shelf to land on the floor of the wash three feet away from him. Nordic stepped out from under the shelf, straightening, swinging around and raising the Yellowboy. The two Half-Moon men, both clad in dusters, stood on the side of the ridge ten feet above the shelf. Seeing him they stopped abruptly and raised their own rifles, one of them yelling a startled curse.

Anders's Yellowboy roared, bucking in his gloved hands.

The bore tore into the chest of the man on the right, who screamed, dropped to his knees and rolled down the side of the ridge toward Nordic. Anders ejected the spent, smoking shell, levered another one into the breech, and fired once more an eyeblink after the second man had fired his own carbine. As the man's bullet tore into the top of the shelf before Anders, Anders's own bullet ripped into the man's lower right side.

The man cursed and dropped his carbine.

Clutching his bloody side, he swung around and ran up the ridge, crouching, moving heavily. Nordic sent two more rounds toward him—one plumed clay dirt and sand ahead of him and slightly right while the second one slammed into the side of the ridge at his heels. He threw himself onto the top of the ridge and rolled out of sight.

"Dammit!" Anders began climbing the ridge to the right of the shelf, crouching low.

He moved slowly, knowing another bullet or two could be coming soon from the top of the ridge. He took one slow step at a time, squeezing the Winchester in his hands. Near the top of the ridge, Anders removed his hat, dropped it, then crawled to the top of the ridge, edging a look over the lip onto the crest. The third man sat back against the rock behind which he and the second man had fired from.

His lower right side was matted with blood oozing out of his brown leather vest, between the flaps of his duster. He held a Schofield .44 in his right hand. Grimacing, breathing hard, he tried to raise it, but it came up only inches from his right thigh. He tossed it away and said, "Don't shoot me!"

Nordic climbed up on top of the ridge and walked toward the wounded man, keeping the Yellowboy aimed at him.

The man stared at him fearfully.

Long, pale hair hung down over his shoulders.

A thick mustache mantled his upper lip.

"Don't shoot an unarmed man," he pleaded. "Ehrlich sent us. We were just doin' our job!"

Nordic stopped before him, the Yellowboy aimed at the man's head.

"So am I," he said.

The Yellowboy roared.

The bullet tore into the man's forehead, above his right eye.

He jerked and slumped to the ground on his right side.

CHAPTER TWENTY

The next morning, Nordic removed the coffeepot from the range and poured the strong, steaming, black liquid into two tin cups. Right after he'd risen from his bed on the floor, he'd let Finn out to hunt his breakfast. Quite the rabbit hunter, that one.

On the cot, holding Robert against her chest, Sarah stirred. She sat up and looked at Nordic who was just then setting the pot back on the range. "I should be making the coffee!"

"Don't be silly. You have Robert to tend."

"But I'm living here free of charge!"

"What? You expect me to make you pay rent?"

"I would gladly…if I had any money…"

"Here." Anders held one of the smoking cups out to her. "Drink that. Then I'll whip up some bacon and eggs, and we'll head to town."

It was Sarah's turn to frown. "Town?"

"Obviously, it's not safe here for you and the baby." Nordic sat at the table and turned his cup so that the handle was on the right side. He lifted the cup and blew on it. "I'm going to put you up at the Dancing Bear in Camp Collins until I can figure out what to do with you."

"What do you mean 'figure out what to do with me'?"

He sipped his coffee and shrugged. "You can't stay here. Like I said, it's not safe. Besides, I'll be pushin' on soon. I don't let much grass grow under my feet."

"Oh." Sarah stared down at her coffee. She seemed sad. She looked at him. "I don't...I don't suppose—"

"There's any way we could stay together? No."

She drew her mouth corners down.

"Don't worry. I'll arrange something."

"Fiddle-footed, aren't you?"

Nordic took another sip of his coffee. "Yes." He stared at her as she again stared pensively into her coffee. "Don't worry," he said. "I'll arrange something for you. I'm not abandoning you and Robert. I know a few people. I'll find you a home."

Again, she turned her mouth corners down.

"Can Robert make it to town on Apache's back?"

"I think so," she said. "He's strong."

Nordic took another sip of his coffee then rose from his chair, set an iron skillet on the range, and lay several strips of bacon in it. When the bacon was half cooked, he took four eggs from a tin bowl and cracked them into the popping skillet.

He looked at Sarah. She was still staring with a sad air into her cup.

Dammit, Anders thought.

A fter breakfast, he saddled Apache and led him around to the front of the cabin. He fetched Sarah, the blanket-wrapped baby, and a carpetbag of supplies for her, and they mounted up. Nordic was afraid the ride might be hard on the boy, but he slept peacefully in Sarah's arms—she sat ahead of Anders in the saddle—most of the way.

They rode into town around noon, and Nordic paid for a room for Sarah and the baby at the Dancing Bear Saloon & Restaurant. He helped her and the baby get situated and then asked for the list of supplies he'd had her write for him back at the line shack before they'd left.

She gave a strained expression as she handed him the scrap of lined notepaper.

"Are you sure?" she said.

"I'm sure." He smiled and left.

He'd just drawn her door closed behind him when a door across the hall and one door up from Sarah's opened and Alexandra stepped out, her hair still damp from a recent bath.

She frowned at Anders. "Following me? Father would have you bullwhipped if he found out." She quirked an ironic smile.

Nordic gave an ironic chuff and shook his head. "I brought Sarah and the baby here. Too dangerous out where I live."

"Where's your loyal companion?"

"At the end of town. Like me, he's right unsociable."

She nodded. "What's in your hand?"

"A list of things Sarah needs for her and the baby."

Alexandra held out her hand. "Let me see."

He reluctantly gave her the list, feeling the heat of embarrassment rise in his cheeks.

Alexandra read the list and laughed. "I'll take care of it. My treat. You'll be run out of town if you're seen buying women's bloomers and baby diapers."

Nordic chuckled. "All right. I'll take you up on that. I don't want to spend another night in jail."

"Buy a girl a drink?"

Nordic shook his head. "A bullwhipping doesn't sound all that inviting."

"No, I suppose not."

"How long are you going to be in town?"

"No telling. I'm thinking of heading back East."

"Your father loves you."

"He thinks he owns me."

"All fathers think they own their daughters."

"I don't like it."

"Do me another favor, will you?"

She smiled saucily. "My bed's made but I can pull the covers back down."

Ignoring the flirtation, he said, "Keep an eye on Sarah for me, will you?"

"Of course." She turned and headed for the stairs, glancing over her shoulder at him with a coquettish look.

He heaved a deep sigh. "That girl's gonna kill me yet."

He let her get a good way away from him then headed for the stairs himself. In the main drinking and eating hall, he saw Bitterman sitting with three bearded, roughhewn men. They were drinking and playing cards. Bitterman was looking at the outside door and then turned to see Nordic staring at him.

Glowering, more like.

Nordic walked over to Bitterman's table and leaned down, giving the Comanche foreman a direct, threatening look.

"Stay away from her. Understand?"

Flushing, Bitterman pinched up his face and narrowed his eyes. "You go to hell!"

Nordic slapped him with the back of his hand.

As Bitterman fell out of his chair, the bearded man to Anders's right yelled, "Hey!" and rose from his own chair.

Nordic sent him to the floor in similar fashion.

One of the other two men dropped his hand beneath the table and hardened his jaws.

Anders leaned toward him, saying with no little threat in his low, even voice, "Go ahead. I'd like you to."

The man froze in his chair. He flushed and slowly lifted his hand onto the table.

Bitterman rose to his feet, his hand over the large, red welt on his cheek. Sitting back down in his chair, hatless, he glared at Nordic. "One of these days, Dakota, you an' me are gonna dance!"

"Why wait? You an' me can do-si-do right now!"

Bitterman just glared at him, flushed with embarrassment. The room had gone deadly quiet—all the other drinkers and diners had heard.

Nordic headed for the door, keeping an eye on the four men in the backbar mirror. He knew none of them was above shooting a man in the back—especially Bitterman.

He went out and stepped up onto Apache's back. They headed out of town. Finn sat where Nordic had left him. When he saw his trail companion, the dog rose, wagged his tail, and gave a happy bark.

"Come on, Finn!" Anders called as if he needed to. "Let's get the hell out of this perdition!"

Finn barked again and ran along beside him and Apache.

They'd ridden for an hour up the Poudre Canyon when Nordic got the sense he was being followed. He continued up along the trail beside the dramatically flowing Poudre River, passing rapids after rapids, rising into thick aspens and pines. When he came to a rocky stretch of trail, where Apache would leave few prints, he swung left off the trail and rose up onto a high, stone escarpment.

At the edge of the scarp, he reached back into his saddlebags and produced his spyglass. He waited until he spied movement on the distant trail below, then raised the glass to his eye. The four riders stopped at where the trail turned to rocks. Nordic grinned.

Sure enough, Bitterman and his cronies. They were following him, probably hoping to bushwhack him.

"Don't they ever learn?" Anders said as he continued staring into the glass.

Finn looked up at him and growled.

"They're just stupid—that's all."

Finn moaned.

"I know, I know," Nordic said, chuckling. "You'd like to take off another toe."

When the four riders continued up the trail, Anders, the dog, and Apache rode south into the high country, taking a shortcut back to the line shack.

He'd be back out tonight, watching the trail out from the Comanche headquarters, intending to follow Bitterman to wherever he rode so late at night.

Up to no good, the man from Dakota had no doubt. But then, few were.

————

"Uh-oh," Nordic said an hour later as he sat atop the slope west of the line shack, just above his swimming hole. "More company!"

A good dozen riders were coming down the ridge behind the cabin and the stable. He could see them making their way through the pines and firs.

"Come on, Finn!" Quickly, he turned Apache around and rode partway down the slope, hoping he hadn't been seen.

He stopped the Appy twenty feet from the top of the slope, muttering, "Sure am glad Sarah and little Robert aren't here."

He swung down from the leather, dropped the

reins, shucked his rifle from its boot, and ran crouching back up the slope. Six feet from the top, he got down and crawled. Near the top he removed his *sombrero* and edged a look over the rise's crest toward the cabin. The riders were just then reaching the bottom of the ridge. There were over a dozen of them if you counted the three dead men slumped across their saddles.

The men who'd pestered Sarah and whom Nordic had sent to their makers. The oldest man in the bunch was no doubt Frank Ehrlich clad in a buffalo coat and wearing a low-crowned black hat. His sun-darkened face was carpeted in a gray beard. The group came up the cabin's east side, swung around the front corner, and turned their mounts to face the cabin itself. They all had their rifles out and resting across their saddle pommels or sticking straight up from their thighs.

Ehrlich, astride a big black horse with three white socks was in the middle of the group, nearest the cabin's front door. He held a Henry repeater in the port arms position across his chest.

"Dakota!" he shouted. "You in there?"

He waited. When no response came from the cabin, Ehrlich rose up straight in his saddle and barked, "Nordic! We wanna talk to you, Nordic! We got some of your handiwork out here!"

Nordic chuckled a dry laugh. "He makes it sound like I killed those three devils in cold blood. Like hell!"

Lying belly flat beside him, Finn raised his hackles and growled.

"Shh, boy. Easy."

The dog lowered his hackles and pulled his lips down over his teeth.

"Nordic, you in there?" Ehrlich shouted again. "You cowering like a cold snake? I don't cotton to my men bein' killed! They're loyal to me an' I'm loyal to them!"

Nordic chuckled again. "He's so full o' crap he'll float away!"

Beside Anders, Finn gave a barely audible yip.

Nordic squeezed his rifle, snaked it low over the top of the slope. The door wasn't locked. The only time it was was when he was inside and had the bar resting in its brackets. The Half-Moon men were liable to break in. If they did that…and not finding him there…they were liable to burn the place down.

They had to get even some damn way…

Ehrlich turned his head to the right and said, "Palmer, Crantz, check it out!"

Nordic gently racked a round into the Yellowboy's breech.

One of the men turned his head toward him and said, "There he is!"

Nordic's heart thudded. "Damn, he's got good ears!"

As the Half-Moon men turned their horses toward him, he pulled the Yellowboy down, depressed the hammer, donned his hat, and scrambled to his feet.

"Come on, Finn. It's about to get hot out here!"

The dog on his heels, he ran to Apache.

CHAPTER TWENTY-ONE

The dog following close on Apache's heels, the trio made good time galloping through a swale then climbing a near ridge. Nordic figured he'd be hard to track on the ridge due to the thin, pine-needle-littered soil.

Besides, he knew the terrain well and knew where he could hole up. This was ancient Comanche and Arapaho range. He doubted the Half-Moon men were out here that much. He crested the ridge, rode down the other side and angled into a broad canyon. When he reached the canyon floor, he halted the Appy under a ledge of rock and glanced up the canyon wall. The thuds of many riders reached his ears, growing louder before dwindling. The Half-Moon men had ridden on past the canyon.

Anders booted Apache out from the ledge and away from the canyon wall, away from where the riders had passed. He found a cave he'd discovered looking for herd-quitting beeves. He led Apache inside, Finn following. The cave was roughly thirty feet deep. He led the horse to the back wall then walked up to the cave entrance, sat down Indian style, and rested the Yellowboy across his lap. Finn sat down beside him and stared out of the cave and to the canyon floor.

He worked his nose, sniffing and shifting his weight from one front paw to the other.

Nordic likely wasn't out of the woods yet, but if they tracked him here, he had at least half a chance of holding them off with the Winchester. He sat waiting and watching and sharing his jerky with Finn, who gobbled it hungrily. At good dark, he left the cave, found his way out of the canyon and back to the line shack.

He was surprised the Half-Moon devils weren't waiting for him.

They'd come for him again, though. He was sure of that.

He tended Apache, and he and Finn went into the shack. He made some coffee, laced it with busthead, and sat at the table in the dark. Finn snored softly on the rug in the parlor area. Wanting to give the horse and the dog a good rest, he waited until the next night to ride over to the Comanche Ranch and waited in the dark beside the trail.

He waited an hour, then two.

Finally, the thuds of a horse sounded.

Finn pricked his ears.

"Easy, boy," Anders whispered.

Up the trail, a jostling shadow appeared. As the

horse and rider approached, Nordic could make out the tall frame of Wayne Bitterman as the man passed Nordic's hidden position along the trail, dust rising in the pale light of the high-kiting moon. When horse and rider had passed, Anders reined Apache onto the trail and followed the Comanche foreman, the man and horse's figures silhouetted in the moonlight.

The man rode for an hour, slowing his horse occasionally to rest it. Nordic did the same with Apache and Finn. Bitterman swung off the main trail onto an old Indian hunting trail that had become a cow path. Nordic followed the man for another forty-five minutes and into a slender canyon in which a low-slung cabin sat on the far side of a creek glistening in the firelight.

He heard the strident lowing of cattle.

"I just had me a feelin'," Nordic said to himself as he reined up behind a broad-boled aspen, on the near side of the lapping creek. He watched Bitterman dismount, tie his reins at the hitchrack, and disappear into the cabin in which two front windows shone with guttering lamplight.

"One of Deveraux's other line shacks," Nordic said again to himself. "And I bet a herd of his beef is in a pen in the back…" He turned to the horse and the dog and said, "You two stay here. I'm gonna check it out."

He gave them both a pat, shucked his Winchester and, moving slowly, crouching, waded the shallow stream. He hoped Bitterman's horse wouldn't give him away. He walked far around the mount's right side. The horse whickered but didn't whinny.

Nordic ducked under a window on the shack's right side, removed his *sombrero*, and edged a look inside. Six men including Bitterman sat around a large table, smoking, drinking whisky, and playing what appeared to be poker. Nordic could hear them through the window. They were palavering and drinking, conversing in jeering tones before Bitterman blew out cigarette smoke, chuckled, and said, "Ehrlich will accept the cattle now that the brands is changed. He'll take 'em down south and sell 'em for a purty penny to a rancher who don't mind a little stolen beef. Rancher from Durango."

The others chuckled.

So Bitterman and his long-looping pards were rustling his boss's own cattle, selling them to Frank Ehrlich at the Half-Moon. I just knew there was a crooked stench on him. Meanwhile, he's set his hat for the boss's daughter…

Anders grimaced his distaste for both Bitterman and Ehrlich.

He considered kicking the door in and gunning Bitterman and the rest of the rustlers. But the fore-man's horse might alert them. Besides, Anders wanted to know where Ehrlich was taking them. Whomever he was selling them to was likely responsible for more long-loopings in the Never Summers.

Some Mex…

Such a man needed to be stopped. Nordic was indignant that they'd rustled the cattle under his own nose and were holding them on Comanche Mountain graze.

Getting careless, old son…

A low growl sounded in the dust behind Anders.

He whipped around and saw two bright yellow eyes glowing in the darkness. He saw the big square head and sharply pricked ears, the lithe body slinking toward him.

Mountain lion!

The big cat growled again, louder.

He was here for the beef, but he likely wouldn't mind a human side dish.

"Damn!"

The cat was fifteen feet away from him. The sweet, wild stench made his eyes water.

The cat moved closer.

Anders didn't want to shoot, but he had to. The cat would pin him up against the cabin wall and rip him to shreds. Behind the cabin, the cattle were lowing anxiously, stirring about. Bitterman's horse pulled at its reins and gave a shrill whinny.

"Damn, is that cat back?" yelled one of the men in the shack.

The cat lunged. Nordic drilled two fast rounds into it.

"Someone's out there!" shouted a man in the cabin.

Pounding footsteps sounded. Someone knocked over a bottle in his haste.

Nordic ran around behind the shack where the lowing of the cattle was almost deafening.

"Well, the cat's dead," one of the men said in humorous air. "Who do you suppose is out here?"

Wayne Bitterman's voice said tightly, "I know who

it is. Oh, I know!" He paused then yelled, "Dakota, I know you're out here. An' you ain't leavin'. Not by a long shot!"

Nordic was outgunned once more, and it was dark. He ran out from the cabin and ran around to the far side of the corral filled with the large, shadowy shapes of heifers. When he saw the rustlers moving out from the cabin and to either side of the corral, intending to circle around Anders and get him in a whipsaw, he ran out from the corral and into the brush sheathing a dry wash.

One of the long-loopers fired. The bullet plunked into a tree a foot to Nordic's right. He leaped into the wash and ran to his left, following the meandering floor of the ravine. Guns barked behind him but none of the bullets came close. The rustlers were enraged and firing without having a target. They were also desperate, panicked. They didn't want their ploy to become known to Deveraux.

Guns continued barking. When the bullets were cutting into the floor of the wash around him, Nordic stopped and whipped around, dropping to a knee. He raised the Yellowboy to his shoulder and cut loose, snapping off three quick rounds. The shadowy figure of a man just then leaping from the brushy bank into the ravine yelped and fell backward, writhing.

Another shadowy figure dropped into the wash. The rustler swung around, dropping to a knee and raising a rifle. Nordic's Winchester spoke again. This man yelped and fell back on the body of his partner.

"Two down," Nordic said, rising and running along

the floor of the wash, staying close to the shadow of the wash's left wall. "Four to go…"

More guns spoke behind him. Out the corners of his eyes he saw the orange flames stabbing from gun maws. He whipped around a bend in the floor of the wash. Three bullets slammed into the embankment on his right, three and four feet away. He ran around the bend and dropped to a knee.

"Get him, Donny," he heard a man say.

"*You* get him, Rube! He already dropped two of us!"

"If we don't get that SOB, we're all gonna be low-hangin' fruit from a pine tree! We'll be right behind you…coverin' you."

"Yeah, right," said the first man with an ironic chuff.

Nordic waited, crouching, squeezing the Yellowboy in his hands.

Footsteps sounded, boots crunching gravel.

The man's shadowy figure appeared. He stepped slowly around the bend in the ravine floor. Nordic saw his hat, neckerchief, and the rifle he held straight out from his right hip. Moonlight glinted off the rifle's breech.

Anders rose quickly.

The man swung toward him, yelling, startled.

Before he could get a shot off, Nordic's rifle leaped and roared, drilling a round into the man's chest. As the man flew back off his heels, he fired a round skyward then dropped with a plunk and a groan. He reached for his rifle.

Anders finished him with another round.

The man's head dropped with another plunk. He sighed as he died.

Down the wash, another man cursed.

"Maybe we oughta wait till morning," another man said quietly, his voice faintly trilling with apprehension.

"Might be too late by morning," another man said. "He's right around the bend. *Shoot!*"

Rifles roared. Nordic saw the flashes from the gun maws.

He swung around and ran up the ravine. He ran hard, holding the Winchester down low along his right leg. His right boot caught on a root growing up from the ravine floor. He fell hard and rolled, dropping his rifle.

He cursed, reached for the Yellowboy and half sat up.

Guns flashed and roared.

A bullet tore into his left shoulder. A punch and searing pain.

Grimacing, he twisted around on his butt, raised the Yellowboy, and returned fire, the Winchester bucking in his hands. He saw the shadows of the men behind him scramble for cover. Grimacing against the pain in his shoulder, Anders hunkered down behind a large rock.

He snaked the Winchester around the side of the rock and waited. A hatted head poked up behind a hump of ground. Nordic fired. The man grunted and cursed as the bullet grazed him. He rose and ran, crouching, holding a hand over his left ear.

Nordic's vision swam from blood loss. He drew back behind the rock and rested against it. He grew weak and was afraid he'd pass out. He must have done just that for a minute or two. Vaguely, he heard footsteps growing louder. When he opened his eyes, Wayne Bitterman was staring down at him, aiming a carbine at him.

"Well, well, Dakota. You don't look too good." His teeth shone in the darkness when he smiled. "No one's ever gonna see you again ceptin' the coyotes and wolves."

There was a low growling and the sound of running, padded feet.

Bitterman frowned and started to turn to look behind him. Nordic saw Finn leap onto the man. Bitterman screamed and dropped his rifle.

"*No!*" he cried. *"Get off me, you cur!"*

He cursed and threw the dog off him.

Finn dropped, yipped, and rolled.

Bitterman staggered toward the dog and drew his pistol.

Nordic shot him in the back of the head.

CHAPTER TWENTY-TWO

The maneuver about killed him with his wounded shoulder, but Nordic lifted Bitterman onto his horse, tied him belly down, and headed for the Comanche headquarters. He'd stuffed his neckerchief into the wound and fashioned a sling for his arm.

He'd checked out Finn and found the dog relatively unharmed. He'd likely just be sore for a few days is all. Nordic himself was in unholy misery, but he'd been in it before. He'd ride to the Comanche and let Deveraux know about his foreman's operation and the stolen cattle. In the morning, after a good night's sleep—he chuckled, sleep like hell—he'd ride to town and rustle up a sawbones.

He, Finn, and Apache rode into the Comanche headquarters an hour later. All the windows were dark. He rode up to the main lodge and cleared his throat though he hadn't had to. A night picket was sitting on a bench to the right of the bunkhouse door.

"Who the hell are you?" he yelled, loudly cocking

a round into his rifle's breech. "Name yourself or I'll shoot you out of the saddle!"

Finn growled at him.

"It's Nordic. I have a special gift for Deveraux."

The man rose from his chair and walked up to the house. As he did, lamps in several of the lodge's windows were painted with flickering lamplight. The big main door opened and the big, gray-headed Deveraux stepped onto the porch, tying the belt of a red plain robe around his waist.

The night picket cursed loudly as he lifted Bitterman's head by a handful of hair.

"It's Bitterman!" he said.

Deveraux frowned, puzzled.

Anders said, "He was rustling your beef for the Half-Moon with five others. The beef's in the corral of your nearest line shack."

"Bitterman was rustling my beef?"

"And selling it to the Half-Moon."

"He's dead as a post," the picket told his boss.

The rancher tugged on his chin whiskers. "I'll be damned…right under my nose."

"Mine, too, I'm afraid."

Alexandra stepped out of the lodge, drawing a powder blue robe closed and frowning curiously into the night where Finn sat beside Nordic and Apache. "Anders…" she said, incredulous.

Finn yipped a greeting at the young woman.

"Anders, what…what…"

"He killed my foreman," her father told his daughter.

"What was he doing?" Alexandra asked Nordic.

"Rustling," Deveraux answered for Anders.

"I just knew it!" Alexandra intoned, holding a hand over her mouth. She glanced at her father. "I told you to be suspicious of him," she admonished.

"One got away. I've never seen him before, but I think he like the others including Bitterman ride…er, rode…for the Half-Moon. There's gonna be trouble."

"Oh, there'll be trouble, all right," Deveraux said, scowling.

"What are you doing here, Alexandra?" Nordic asked.

"I came out to get some medicine for little Robert. My mother made her own, and it's the best. I'll head back to town in the morning."

She glanced sheepishly at her father, who said, "Oh, Alexandra. You're just trying to make me mad!"

"Not tough to do, Father." She started down the porch steps, frowning up at Anders. "You're hurt."

"Took a blue whistler. I'll have it tended in town."

"No, you won't. I'll tend it here. Come inside." She looked at the night picket. "Mel, tend his horses, will you? And Bitterman."

"Alexandra, I'll give my men their orders." Deveraux turned to the night picket. "Mel, tell the men to ride out at first light. I want those cattle back."

"Well, now you don't have to." She looked up at Nordic again. "Come inside, Anders, before you bleed out."

Nordic looked at Deveraux. "Do you mind?"

"What good would it do if I did? My daughter is a strong-willed woman who lives to gall me."

Nordic dismounted and shucked his rifle. He handed both sets of reins to Mel, said, "Stay, Finn," and started up the porch steps.

Finn whined.

Anders followed the woman inside and into the kitchen. He leaned the rifle in a corner. Deveraux headed upstairs to bed, yawning and saying, "You two be good down here. I have a double barrel in my room!"

Alexandra took a bottle of Scotch whisky off a shelf and set it with a water glass on the table.

"Have a seat," she said to Nordic, pulling a chair out and angling it toward Anders. "Have some hooch. That wound has to hurt like blazes."

"Blazes doesn't do it justice."

She pumped water into a kettle and set it on the range. She pulled some cloths out of a drawer and said, "I'll be back."

She left the kitchen. Anders could hear her climbing the stairs. She returned a few minutes later and set a canvas sewing pouch on the table.

"Ouch," Nordic said.

Alexandra poured the warm water into a basin and added whisky from the bottle.

"That's kind of top-shelf for medicine, ain't it?" Nordic asked.

"Aside from Spanish brandy, it's all we have."

Anders chuckled. "Don't doubt it a bit."

She removed the sling and then his shirt and went

to work cleaning the wound. His pronounced muscles and tendons across his chest, belly, and shoulders writhed with the pain spasms. The whisky burned but he was glad he was getting the wound cleaned. He likely would have passed out on the way to town.

Alexandra didn't say anything for a long time until she said, "You should ask my father for Wayne's job."

"I work alone. Besides, I wouldn't get it…because of you."

Her cheeks colored as she continued cleaning the wound. He stared at her. What a beauty, he reflected. And off-limits. It saddened him a little, but they belonged to two different worlds. Besides, Nordic was a loner. He could live with only a dog.

He sipped his whisky. "That is not bad," he said.

Alexandra gave an ironic snort.

She finished cleaning and bandaging the wound and gave him his bloodstained shirt. "You'll need a new one of these. I'd give you one of Father's but it wouldn't fit a man your size."

She helped him put it on and button it, then replaced the sling. She set another glass on the table and poured the Scotch into it. She sat at the end of the table and sipped the whisky. She stared at him for a time, running a long, slender finger around the rim of the glass.

"Sarah's in love with you," she said.

Nordic pulled his mouth corners down and shook his head. Sarah had told him the same about Alex.

She sipped her whisky again and said, "Must be rough, having so many women in love with you."

He chuckled.

"What are you going to do when you leave here?"

"I never know until I do it."

"What a life, Anders."

He shrugged. "I like it."

"You could stay in the shack. Father needs someone to watch the herds all the time."

He looked at her and smiled. "Too dangerous for you *and* him. In case you hadn't noticed, I attract trouble."

"Coward."

"What are you going to do?" he asked her.

She sighed. "I reckon I'll know when I do it."

"Stay here, Alex. He needs you. Whether you believe it or not, you need him. If not, you wouldn't have come. Besides, you're a part of this country."

She sighed. "Yes, that's the trouble." She looked at him from beneath her brows, hands wrapped around her goblet. "You're the first man I ever loved."

"I'm sorry."

"I'll always remember you."

"I'm sorry."

"Stop saying that. Why do you hate that I love you."

"Because I feel the same way and it's not good for us."

Her cheeks colored.

Out a window, Nordic saw lights in the bunkhouse. It was nearly dawn. The men were likely rustling up a quick breakfast and would be heading out soon. Nordic should be riding out, too, and get to work on the range. He'd messed up in letting those beeves get rustled and he felt the need to redeem himself. On the other hand, he didn't want to leave Alexandra and her father alone here.

Trouble in the form of the Half-Moon riders would come eventually. One of the men Nordic had hunted had gotten away, so Ehrlich likely knew by now that Deveraux knew about the rustling, and he might want to make the first move against his rival.

"Breakfast?" Alexandra asked Nordic.

"Sure."

She finished her drink and rose, headed for the range. "I'll stir up some antelope sausage and eggs. That's Father's favorite."

Nordic now had a reason to stay.

Good.

Besides, he was so hungry his stomach thought his throat had been cut. He watched Alexandra cook but quickly averted his gaze when her father entered the kitchen. Too late. Anders had been caught.

"Mind your eyes, boy!" Deveraux admonished and poured himself a drink.

Anders's cheeks warmed. Alexandra glanced over her shoulder at him, smiling.

They'd eaten and washed the antelope and potatoes down with more whisky and coffee when Finn started barking angrily in the yard.

"Damn," Nordic said.

He rose from his chair and grabbed his rifle. He stepped out onto the porch and saw Finn standing near the bunkhouse, staring down the trail to the east. His hackles were raised, and his tail was arched. With each angry bark, his front feet rose from the ground.

Nordic whistled and the dog came running.

As he did, Anders heard the rataplan of galloping hooves. Riders were coming fast from the valley of the Avalanche River below. Deveraux came out of the house, holding a double-barreled twelve gauge up high across his chest.

"If that don't sound like Ehrlich, nothing does!"

Finn was on the deck, standing beside Nordic. He pointed off to his left and said, "Finn." He didn't want the dog in a possible cross fire.

Alexandra came out of the house holding a Winchester at port arms, as well, her cheeks flushed, eyes wide with anxiety.

"Is there a back door?" Anders asked Deveraux.

The man nodded.

"I'm gonna circle around."

The rancher jiggled extra shells in his pants pocket.

As Nordic went inside, Deveraux turned to his daughter. "Alexandra, get inside and get your head down."

"Nope."

Nordic heard the rancher give a frustrated chuff.

The hoof thuds grew louder and fell silent as he heard Ehrlich's raspy, belligerent voice say, "Whoa! Whoa!" Then: "Deveraux, I'm short four men!"

"I'm short twenty heifers!" Deveraux returned.

Nordic came up close against the side of the house, moving furtively. He held the Yellowboy straight up and down against his chest.

"Where's your line rider?" Ehrlich barked at Deveraux.

"Right here!" Nordic stepped out from the corner of the house, aiming the Yellowboy at the dozen, hard-faced men sitting their horses in front of the lodge. They all had their own rifles in hand and aimed at the lodge. Nordic said, "Tell your men to drop their rifles...you, too, Ehrlich...or I'll blow *you* out of your saddle!"

Ehrlich glared at him from under the brim of his low-crowned black hat that like its owner had seen better days. His eyes flattened with apprehension. His craggy cheeks flushed beneath his thin beard.

"Ready to shovel coal?" Nordic asked him.

Deveraux winced, cursed.

"Drop them!" Deveraux bellowed.

"Pistols, too," ordered Nordic.

The men looked around at each other. Ehrlich stared down the maw of Nordic's Yellowboy. Then he dropped his Winchester and followed it with his six-shooter. He looked at the men to either side of him. "Drop 'em, boys, or you're all gonna be ridin' the grub line right fast."

Reluctantly, they all pulled their pistols from their holsters and dropped them to the ground.

"Now, get the hell out of here!" Deveraux shouted, holding his double-bore on the Half-Moon men.

Ehrlich cursed, reined his horse around, then galloped out of the yard. His men followed suit, glaring at Nordic over their shoulders. Hooves drummed as they galloped down into the valley of the

Avalanche River. The drumming dwindled and then they were gone.

Nordic walked around to the front of the house and mounted the porch where Deveraux and his daughter stood, still holding their shotgun and rifle, respectively.

"They'll be back," Deveraux said grimly.

"Want me to stay?"

Deveraux shook his head. "They won't come back today. They need to rearm and rest their horses. Ehrlich doesn't have a large remuda. I'll take my men and head over to the Half-Moon in a day or two. My men outnumber his. He'll be taught what happens when you long-loop Comanche beef."

Nordic nodded. "I'll get to work, then."

"Be careful, Anders," Alexandra said.

Again, Nordic nodded. He shouldered his rifle and started walking down to the stable to Apache.

Behind him, Deveraux said, "Nordic?"

Anders turned back to him.

"Thanks," the rancher said.

Nordic whistled for Finn and continued to the stable, the dog running along by his side.

CHAPTER TWENTY-THREE

Nordic finished out the day on Comanche range then returned to the line shack, took a swim in the creek to clean himself up and, shivering against the creek's frigid chill, toweled off, mounted up, and rode to town. He left Finn at the edge of the settlement and rode over to the Dancing Bear.

He wanted to check on Sarah and the baby.

He went inside and upstairs to Sarah's room and knocked on the door. It was Alexandra who answered his knock, clad in blue jeans and wool work shirt but looking as beautiful as ever. Her hair was partly pinned up on her head.

"Come in," she said. "I just gave little Robert some of my mother's old recipe and I think his temperature is already starting to break."

Nordic stepped into the room, removing his hat.

Sarah sat at a table by the room's only window, holding the blanket-wrapped baby in her arms. There was worry in her eyes, but it was tempered by hope.

"I was so worried," she told Anders. "The doctor here isn't much good. I smelled alcohol on his breath. I think Alexandra might have saved little Bob."

He glanced at Alexandra. "She ain't just a purty picture."

Sarah smiled.

Alexandra flushed.

"What are you doing in town?" Sarah asked him.

"I wanted to check on you an' little Bob, as you call him. I've been worried." He paused. "Have either of you eaten?"

Both Alexandra and Sarah shook their heads.

"Let's go downstairs and I'll buy us a meal. Can li'l Bob be alone for a while? I think you need a break."

Sarah nodded. "He'll just sleep. It would be nice to leave the room."

"Let's go," Nordic said.

They went down, sat at a table in the middle of the drinking and eating hall, which was nearly empty on this weeknight. They ordered food and coffee and ate. When they'd finished with the main meal, they ordered dried peach pie and more coffee. They were just finishing dessert when an obviously drunk man— tall and beefy and bearded—staggered over to their table. He was as ugly as leftover sin, a large wart bristling above the bridge of his nose.

"Ah, Dakota," he said, slurring his words, "I see you got you some purty little fillies...even a man as big and ugly as you..."

Nordic didn't know the man from Adam's off ox.

Obviously, Nordic's reputation had preceded him as it often did. He could see the man was drunk and trolling for a fight.

"Skedaddle," Nordic said softly.

Alexandra and Sarah regarded him anxiously.

The big man pointed at Alexandra. "That there is Deveraux's daughter. Does he know you're cavortin' with his princess? If not, I bet he'd like to know."

He laughed, jeeringly.

Nordic was about to stand. Alexandra held him down by placing a hand on his thigh. She canted her head toward Sarah and the baby.

Anders settled back into his seat though his blood was boiling.

The troublemaker looked at Sarah. "Or maybe it's the sweet little thing. Is that your child, Dakota?" He grinned lewdly at Sarah, who held little Robert close against her breast. "I bet she was fun. The young ones usually are."

Anders was out of his seat before he knew it. He turned to the big, drunk brigand and smashed his right fist against the man's left cheek, sending him stumbling backward, cursing. He flopped back onto a table from which its two inhabitants scattered after grabbing their beers.

Alexandra gasped. Sarah screamed.

Anders, so enraged he was seeing red, drew the man up by his shirt collar and smashed his fist three more times into the man's face. "You remember this beating when you feel like insulting women or anyone else—understand?"

"Yeah! Yeah! Yeah!"

"Oh, we're not done yet!"

Anders was about to hammer the man's large, round, ugly face once more when a man's voice he recognized as belong to town marshal Glen Conagher said behind him, "Oh, I think you are."

Something hard smashed against the back of Nordic's head.

Then, just before everything went dark, he heard Sarah scream once more.

———

Something cool and rubbery pushed against Nordic's cheek.

A mewling sounded.

Anders opened his eyes, one by one, and winced as the light struck each like javelins.

He canted his gaze to his left. Finn sat beside where he lay on yet another jail cot. Finn was sniffing him and yipping softly, with concern. The door of the cell they were in was closed. The fat deputy sat at the edge of the marshal's desk, running an oily rag along the stock of a handsome Henry repeating rifle.

"Not this again," Nordic said, rising onto his elbows.

The fat deputy looked at him and chuckled. "That dog of yours sure is loyal. I'll give him that."

Nordic rubbed the back of his head on which a goose egg had sprouted. A tender one. There was a cut on it. Anders looked at his fingers. Blood.

"Now, I'll agree—Devine had that beatin' comin'. But Marshal Conagher can't walk into a place where there's a beatin' goin' on and not do anything about it."

Nordic glanced at the empty cells around him. "Where is this Devine fella. I didn't take him to the woodshed for nothin'."

"At the sawbones." The fat deputy chuckled again. "Gettin' his jaw reset. Can hear him howlin' from a block away."

Nordic sat up and set his feet on the floor, one to either side of the doting Finn. "Let me out of here. I have work to do. That SOB was pestering the women."

The fat deputy shook his head. "Conagher says you're goin' before the judge tomorrow mornin' when he arrives here from Gold Mound. Prob'ly hangin' a man even as we speak. Loves a good hangin', the judge does. He might even hang you just fer the fun of it."

"What I did wasn't a hangin' offense."

"The fellas who took Devine over to the sawbones said he was half dead. A brainin' like that"—the deputy shook his head—"ain't good."

Anders stood, went over to the cell door, and squeezed his hands around two steel bars. "Let me out of here, dammit! I told you I have work to do an' that idiot, Devine, deserved every punch I tagged him with!"

Again, the deputy grinned, wagged his head. "Told you—you can't—" He'd just glanced out the window over the desk. He cursed loudly and stopped cleaning the rifle. "Well, I'll be jiggered!"

Keeping his attention on the window, the deputy said, "You sure must have that girl under your spell—I'll give you that!"

Just as footsteps sounded on the porch, the deputy opened the door. Alexandra stepped into the jailhouse and stood before the doorway, arms crossed on her chest, one booted foot cocked forward, lovely head canted to one side, reprovingly.

She didn't say anything. She didn't have to. The deputy sighed and grabbed the large key ring off the support post, saying, "You can't fight town hall an' you can't fight a Deveraux."

The key scraped in the lock. The deputy stepped back as he pulled the door open. Finn gave an excited bark. Nordic grabbed his hat off the cot, set it on his head, and walked out of the cell, Finn close on his heels. As he approached Alexandra, she turned and walked out of the jail office, Nordic behind her, Finn following his trail partner.

"We gotta quit meetin' like this," Nordic said.

"Don't we."

"Uh…sorry…"

"What for? He's a lout. Now that he's had his jaw broken, maybe he'll mind his manners."

"Doubt it."

"Me, too."

"How's Sarah?"

"Sound asleep when I left her and little Bob."

Anders saw his horse and Alexandra's black tied to the hitchrack fronting the jailhouse. He frowned at the young woman, curious. "Where you goin'?"

"Home. An itinerant farrier came into the Dancing Bear a few minutes ago. He pulled me aside and shared some very important...and frightening...information. He'd been shoeing horses at the Half-Moon last night and overheard Ehrlich's plans to ride out and 'lay waste' to the Comanche headquarters at high noon today, when all the hands would be there, and he could kill them all as well as Father and burn down the lodge. I have to warn Father. Will you join me?"

"Of course!" Nordic unwrapped his reins from the hitchrack and swung up into the leather, his right hand wrapping around his rifle butt, glad to find it there.

Alex swung up onto her black.

Nordic said, "Come on, Finn!"

As Anders and the young woman swung their horses out into the street and broke into sudden gallops, heading toward the trail that ran along the canyon of the Cache la Poudre, Finn barked, instantly excited, and ran along beside his two trail partners.

The trail climbed sharply to the left of the river's stormy, frothing waters, between the pine forest and the thundering stream. It took them over an hour to reach the trail that rose then dipped into the canyon of the Avalanche River. They passed the canyon in which the Half-Moon lay and continued south. An hour later, when they were roughly a mile from the trail branching off toward Comanche Mountain and the ranch headquarters, they heard hooves thundering behind them.

Alexandra swung a quick look over her right shoulder.

"It's them!" she cried. "It's Ehrlich and the Half-Moon men!"

Nordic swung his own look over his shoulder. Twelve or so men were galloping toward him and Alexandra, Ehrlich himself in his low-crowned black hat, riding lead.

He turned to yell at the men behind him. "It's Dakota and the Deveraux girl. We'll kill them first!"

Nordic turned to Alexandra. "I got a feelin' he'd take your pa by surprise. Your pa is overconfident and Ehrlich's sneaky."

"What should we do?"

"Lead 'em away from the Comanche. Your pa will hear the gunshots. Come on!"

They both crouched low in their saddles and urged their horses into even more speed, Finn running hard along behind them, barking with excitement.

Nordic turned to Alexandra. "Where's a shallow place to cross the river? I've seen it but just can't remem—"

"Straight ahead another hundred yards!" she yelled above the rataplan of their horses' pounding hooves.

Anders saw it a minute later—the shallow top of a low waterfall tumbling down from rocks, sand, and gravel, on the left side of the trail. They swung their mounts into the river and easily traversed the shallow stretch, water splashing up against their horses' hocks. Finn followed, still barking.

On the other side of the stream, Nordic turned Apache back to face it, saw the riders closing on them along the two-track trail. He shucked the Yellowboy, rammed the butt plate against his shoulder, lined up the sights on one of the riders, and fired.

They were moving too fast, jostling too violently.

His round flew wide, but it wasn't a wasted shot. It not only slowed their pursuers but stopped them. They leaped out of their saddles and ran for cover, yelling and cursing.

Anders said, "Let's go!" and rammed the Winchester into the scabbard. "Come on, Finn!" he called as he and Alexandra galloped straight across the meadow to the east of the river.

Behind them, rifles barked and men shouted in frustration.

Their bullets fell short.

Nordic, Alexandra, and Finn entered the wood a hundred yards south of the river and began climbing the ridge, the pine duff perfuming the air around them.

Alex looked at Nordic. "I know where you're going. It's a good plan!"

"Oh, I'm just full of 'em. Stay with me, kid!"

"Any day of the week, Mister, though I know you're not serious, you cad!"

Anders laughed.

Running close beside him now, Finn barked.

They crested the ridge, hearing the thunder of the Half-Moon horses once more though farther away than before. The thunder was growing steadily louder, though. They were closing the gap between Nordic and Alexandra.

Nordic swung his horse right to gallop along the top of the ridge and soon it appeared—a stone, brush-roofed sheepherder's shack hunkered in the shade of a tall pine.

"We *might* be able to hold 'em off from there," Anders yelled.

"We might." Alex nodded dubiously. "We might…"

CHAPTER TWENTY-FOUR

Nordic thought that when the shooting started in earnest, Deveraux would hear it and he'd order his men into their saddles. This was Comanche range, after all. The only shooting the rancher wanted to hear on his own graze was that of his own men shooting rustlers like ducks on a millpond. He'd come, all right.

But in time?

Nordic and Alexandra pulled up to the old, stone sheepherder's hovel and leaped out of their saddles. They spanked both mounts, sending them galloping around the shack and beyond, not wanting them to get caught in a cross fire. There was still an old but stout wooden front door on the shack, and Nordic opened it and walked into the barren, dirt-floored building rife with mouse droppings and spider webs.

Finn followed them inside, panting, looking up at Nordic as though awaiting instructions.

Sidling up to a glassless window right of the door, Nordic looked down at his loyal companion and said,

"You go curl up in that corner and keep your head down, young man. Like I told you before, you ain't armed and I don't want you gettin' your head blown off. You're my only friend, and I was friendless long enough."

"He's not your only friend," Alexandra said as she sidled up to the window on the other side of the door, which they'd closed though after practically seventy years of the shack being abandoned, it wasn't a very tight fit. Someone could easily kick it open. She pinned Nordic with a serious look. "I'm your friend, Anders. Always."

She hurried over to him and threw her arms around his neck and hugged and kissed him. "We are at least that."

Anders touched his thumb to her nose and winked.

In his corner, Finn gave a quiet yip.

Nordic glanced at the dog and said, "You get your own woman."

Finn mewled and slapped his tail against the earthen floor.

Alex had returned to her window, looking at Nordic. "Am I your woman?"

"Maybe in another life."

"You know most men would kill for me, don't you?"

"Hell, I'd kill for you. But then your pa would kill *me*!" Anders smiled.

He glanced out his window, spied movement in the forest on the other side of the ridge crest. "They're here," he said quietly. "Moving up on us quiet-like."

Alexandra pulled her head back from the window on the other side of the door from Nordic.

"Got plenty of shells for that carbine?"

They'd both pulled their saddlebags off their horses. Hers lay at her feet. She patted it. "This Eastern-educated girl knows how to come to a party."

Nordic chuckled and glanced around the edge of his window again. "There's gonna be shootin' soon. The problem with this place, a slug could ricochet off a rock wall."

"Where else could we go?"

"We'll just have to be lucky I reckon. Hope your pa and his riders get here before we're both toe down."

From his corner, Finn gave a soft yip.

Just then Anders saw one of the Half-Moon riders run out from behind a stout fir and run toward a rock roughly thirty feet out from the front of the cabin.

"Time to get this dance started!" Nordic pumped a round into the Yellowboy's action, aimed quickly but expertly, and fired.

The running man yelped and fell five feet from the rock he'd been heading for, clutching the outside of his right thigh. "Son of a *bitch*!"

Hardening his jaws, Nordic racked another round and finished the Half-Moon rider with a bullet through his chest. The man flopped back down on the ground and lay still.

Frank Ehrlich poked his head out from behind the spruce he used for cover. "You'll pay for that, Dakota. And the princess will, too." Nordic saw him smile lewdly. "Real *slow*."

Nordic fired again. That bullet slammed into the side of the spruce behind which Ehrlich was crouched. The man gave a shrill curse as bark and wood splinters penetrated his eyes just before he drew his head back behind the tree. "You son of a bitch!" the outlaw rancher yelled.

Pumping another round into the Yellowboy's action, Nordic said, "I get it. I'm right popular!"

"Let's shoot him out of there, boss!" one of the rancher's unseen men shouted, his voice hoarse with rage.

Nordic spied movement in the pines, a man switching one covering tree for another a little closer to the shack. Anders drew a bead on him and fired. The man yelped and flew backward down the ridge, dropping his rifle, arms pinwheeling.

"Alex!"

She looked at Anders.

He canted his head to a window at the back of the shack. "Go. Hurry!" He glanced at where Finn sat in a corner behind him. "You, too, Finn—follow Alex!"

"Where am I going?" Alex asked as she ran crouching to the window.

"Outside! Quick! We won't make it in here! I wasn't considering these damn rock walls!"

Alex threw one leg through the window then the other and dropped out of sight. Finn leaped up onto the stone casing at the bottom of the window and turned to Nordic.

"Go, boy!"

Finn barked his reluctance and leaped out the window.

"Shoot 'em outta there!" shouted Ehrlich.

Nordic raised the Yellowboy and emptied the rifle into the pines, hearing one man yelp. Following the yelp, all hell broke loose—rifles blasting, powder smoke wafting from the forest, bullets caroming through the windows, lead spanging off the walls flanking Nordic. He quickly reloaded the Yellowboy and returned fire, nearly emptying the Winchester again while lead buzzed around him and slammed into the stone walls around him.

He wanted to return enough lead that they didn't figure his ploy—to evacuate the cabin before he got filled with so much lead he'd rattle when he walked. He wanted to buy himself, Alex, and Finn enough time to get to relative safety before Ehrlich and his men grew savvy to his ploy.

He wanted to circle around behind the Half-Moon men while they were distracted by their own shooting and take them all from behind. Shoot them all in the back if he had to. They deserved nothing better than to be put down like hydrophobic curs.

He triggered two more rounds into the forest from which smoke wafted thickly. Then, with lead buzzing around his head and slamming into the stone walls around him, he rose and ran to the back window, vaulted off his heels and, holding the Yellowboy in one hand, dove through it headfirst.

He hit the ground hard.

He rolled.

Alexandra and Finn kneeled to his right, Alexandra looking horrified as she stared down at him.

"You're hit, you idiot!"

He looked at himself. Blood shone on his arms and legs, and he felt a nasty burn across his left cheek. He ran his hand across it, looked at it. Blood.

"Well, I'll be damned," he said.

"Why didn't you come out when we did?"

"Wanted to hold 'em off, make 'em believe we were gonna be in there for a while."

Nordic rose, staying away from the window because the Half-Moon fusillade was ongoing, rifles thundering, bullets spanging off the shack's stone walls and threading the air around Nordic, Finn, and Alexandra as they caromed out the window. He grabbed his rifle and looked at the rise fifteen feet behind the shack.

"Come on," he said. "Stay low!"

"Where are we going?" Alex asked, following him, as was Finn.

"We're gonna flank the sonso'bitches!"

They ran up and over the rise, keeping the shack between them and the trigger-happy Half-Moon men. At the bottom of the rise, they swung right and ran into the forest and worked around behind Ehrlich's men who were still triggering lead at the shack. Nordic saw them—nearly a dozen men crouched behind tree boles, on one knee and levering and firing. He saw Ehrlich, farthest man on his left. The rancher was whooping and hollering with bloodbath glee.

The Comanche range would soon be his. Or so he

thought. He was drunk on the idea of usurping Deveraux's position in these mountains.

Nordic, Alex, and Finn crouched behind a spruce bole. Anders said, "Stay here and make sure your rifle's loaded."

"It is."

"Honey," he said, "you're a keeper."

"That's what I've been trying to tell you, you idiot!"

He ran crouching over to a stout pine, racked a round into the Yellowboy's action. Finn followed, hunkered down behind him. Anders glanced at Alex and smiled. He raised his rifle to his shoulder, picked out one of the Half-Moon men, and squeezed the trigger.

The rifle thundered, leaping in his hands.

The man yelped and fell forward with a bullet through his head, just below his hat. He reached for his fallen rifle but then his hand fell still as his lights dimmed and he died. The others swung around suddenly, eyes wide in shock and exasperation. Nordic and Alex's rifles spoke as they fired and jacked fresh rounds...fired and jacked fresh rounds.

They had nearly twenty rounds between them, and neither missed a shot.

The Half-Moon men died hard and fast, only one getting a shot off before Alex drilled him in the belly. He cursed, grabbed his bloody gut, and fell back against the ground, spurs chinging as he shook and expired.

Frank Ehrlich, shot in the leg and shoulder, sank

back against the tree he'd been using for cover. He
blinked several times, wincing against the misery that
Nordic's bullets evoked in his aged body. His eyes
found Nordic walking toward him, holding his rifle
down low against his right leg.

Ehrlich looked from the rifle to the man from
Dakota's hard, flat eyes. Gradually, knowing what was
about to happen, he widened them. The light of
atavistic fear shone in those demonic orbs. The man
from Dakota stopped before the outlaw rancher, five
feet away.

"No," Ehrlich said. "Don't…don't do this. I was…
I was wrong!"

"No," Nordic said. "I was wrong. I should have
killed you the first time I saw you."

"No!"

"Did you really think you were going to wipe out
the Comanche and absorb Deveraux's land?"

Ehrlich looked at Alexandra who'd walked up to
stand beside the man from Dakota. She stared flatly
down at the outlaw rancher who'd likely been
siphoning off her father's beef for years with the inten-
tion of wiping the Deveraux family out once and for
all. Then Ehrlich would be the king of these
mountains.

"I'm…sorry," Ehrlich said. "I just got greedy's
all."

"You're nothing, Ehrlich," Alex said. "Nothing at
all. Just another outlaw holing up in these mountains
that were so much better before you came and that will
be so much better when you're gone."

"You go to hell!"

"You first," Nordic said and raised his rifle.

"No," Alex said, shoving his rifle down. "Let me do it."

"*No, oh Christ!*" Ehrlich pleaded.

Slowly, Alex racked a fresh round into her Winchester's breech. The spent casing clattered onto a rock behind her. She levered a live one into the action and with one hand aimed the Winchester's barrel at Ehrlich's forehead.

"*No!*" the rancher pleaded once more. "I don't wanna die like this!"

He raised his hands as if to ward off the lead and, squeezing his eyes closed, turned his head to one side.

"Oh, yes," Alexandra said. "This is how you were meant to die since the day you were born."

Her Winchester leaped and roared.

Ehrlich's head slammed back against the tree behind him. He gave a deep, last sigh and slid sideways to the ground on one shoulder.

"Good god!" said a voice behind her and Nordic.

Anders swung around to see her father, Garth Deveraux, and a half dozen of his men sitting horses ten feet away. Deveraux stared in astonishment at the dead Ehrlich. His eyes dropped to her smoking rifle and then rose to her face and then slid to Anders. Deveraux looked at the dead men strewn in bloody piles around them.

"What happened here?" he asked.

"Just cleaning up the mountains," Nordic said.

Deveraux looked at the dead rancher and his dead

men once more. "Well...that's one way to skin a cat," he said, finally, wonderingly. "That should take care of my problems." He looked at Alexandra. "I thought you were in town."

"Acquired other plans, Father."

Deveraux thumbed his hat up on his forehead and chuckled dryly. "I see that." He glanced at the men around him. "Head on back to the ranch. This was a wasted trip." To Nordic and his daughter, he said, "Heard the shooting..."

"I figured you would," Anders said.

"Better late than never, Father."

Deveraux gave his head a slow wag as his men reined their horses around and they galloped back down the ridge.

He turned to Alex. "Give me and my line rider a minute here, will you?"

"Of course."

Alex glanced at Nordic then, taking her rifle in one hand, climbed the ridge in search of their horses.

When he and Nordic were alone, Deveraux said, "Do you want her?"

"I can't have her."

"What if you could?"

Nordic thought about that. His head was spinning. He thought about his lonely life, the long, lonely years ahead. Did it have to be that way?

"Yes," he said though he couldn't believe his own ears.

"She comes with a price," Deveraux said.

"Don't they all?"

"She comes with a ranch. If any couple can run the Comanche after I'm gone, it's you two. I'll need grandchildren. Several. That's part of it."

Finn sat mewling beside Nordic, trying to follow the conversation.

"What about him?" Nordic asked, glancing at the shepherd dog.

"He can drink my brandy and smoke my cigars if he wants."

Finn barked his approval.

"All right, then," Nordic said. "If she agrees, then I do, too."

Deveraux smiled, then reined around and spurred his mount into a gallop down the mountain.

Nordic stood in shock for a long time, his mind awhirl at how his life had changed so dramatically, staring down at where the Comanche men had disappeared among the pines. Alexandra rode down to him, leading Apache by his bridle reins. She stopped six feet away and gazed down at him.

"Are you all right?" she asked.

Nordic cleared his throat. "Not…not sure."

She gave a half smile and blinked slowly.

"It'll be all right," she said. "You'll see."

"Are you sure?"

"Oh, yes." She handed him his bridle reins. "Mount up and we'll go home and get those wounds cleaned. We'll get hitched in Camp Collins and start making babies. Don't worry, you can still hunt rustlers. I won't take that away from you"—she glanced at Finn —"and your loyal protector."

Nordic took the reins and walked up to her. She leaned down and kissed him hungrily. She pulled away, smiling. "It won't be so bad. You'll see. We'll make a good team, you an' me." She narrowed her eyes, crossing them slightly in admonishment. "But we have to keep you out of town!"

Nordic laughed, pulled her head down, and kissed her again. Her lips were as sweet as cherries.

They rode down the mountain together, Finn running along behind them, barking.

A LOOK AT:
THE REVENGER OMNIBUS

FROM THE BESTSELLING AUTHOR OF THE SHERIFF BEN STILLMAN NOVELS COMES A BRAND-NEW WESTERN ADVENTURE SERIES.

Mike Sartain, The Revenger, grew up in the French Quarter of New Orleans where he was taught how to fight by some of the toughest, meanest SOBs in any port. He was also taught how to love by some of the most beautiful women in the world.

But after the War Between the States, the former Confederate came west and joined the frontier cavalry. Wounded by Apaches in Arizona, he was nursed back to health by an old desert rat and his beautiful granddaughter, Jewel.

When the prospector and Jewel were viciously murdered by marauding Yankee bluecoats, Mike hunted the soldiers down and killed them one by one—in his own fierce Cajun style. And that's how Mike Sartain's lust for revenge got started. That's how he became a wanted man known as The Revenger and gained a dead-or-alive price on his head.

Now, with no choice but to keep on riding, The Revenger rides for anyone who has an axe to grind.

AVAILABLE NOW

ABOUT THE AUTHOR

Peter Brandvold grew up in the great state of North Dakota in the 1960's and '70s, when television Westerns were as popular as shows about hoarders and shark tanks are now, and Western paperbacks were as popular as *Game of Thrones*.

Brandvold watched every Western series on television at the time. He grew up riding horses and herding cows on the farms of his grandfather and many friends who owned livestock.

Brandvold's imagination has always lived and will always live in the West. He is the author of over one hundred lightning-fast action Westerns under his own name and his pen name, Frank Leslie.

Printed in Dunstable, United Kingdom